acceleration hours

acceleration hours

stories

Jesse Goolsby

UNIVERSITY OF NEVADA PRESS Reno & Las Vegas

University of Nevada Press | Reno, Nevada 89557 USA
www.unpress.nevada.edu
Flame image by Ronald Plett from Pixabay

LIBRARY OF CONGRESS CATALOGING-IN-PUBLICATION DATA

Names: Goolsby, Jesse, author.
Title: Acceleration hours : stories / Jesse Goolsby.
Description: Reno ; Las Vegas : University of Nevada Press,
    [2020] |
  Summary: "Acceleration Hours is a short story collection about
    families, life, and loss set against the backdrop of America's
    wars in the twenty-first century"—Provided by publisher.
Identifiers: LCCN 2019058008 (print) | LCCN 2019058009
    (ebook) | ISBN 9781948908627 (cloth) |
    ISBN 9781948908634 (ebook)
Subjects: LCGFT: Short stories.
Classification: LCC PS3607.O59254 A25 2020 (print) |
    LCC PS3607.O59254 (ebook) | DDC 813/.01083581—dc23
LC record available at https://lccn.loc.gov/2019058008
LC ebook record available at https://lccn.loc.gov/2019058009

FIRST PRINTING

Manufactured in the United States of America

Contents

Acknowledgments

My deepest appreciation for:
Sarah, Ella, Owen, and Abby
Family, friends, colleagues, and readers
University of Nevada Press
Ed Maxwell at Greenburger Associates
United States Air Force Academy, University of
    Tennessee, and Florida State University

The following publications, where these stories previously
appeared in different form:
Narrative Magazine: "Anchor & Knife," "All Saints' Eve,"
    "Hindu Kush"
Blackbird: "We Drag Our Feet near the Stingrays"
Kenyon Review Online: "Feed"
Consequence Magazine: "Tendons"
Redivider: "Sometimes Kids Bleed for No Reason"
TriQuarterly: "God's Zipper"
The Florida Review: "Begin with Serenity"
*Alaska Quarterly Review, I'd Walk with My Friends If
    I Could Find Them* (Houghton Mifflin Harcourt):
    "Waiting for Red Dawn"
Pleiades, Best Small Fictions (2017): "Waist Deep at
    Hapuna"
The Journal, Best of the Net (2015), *I'd Walk with My Friends
    If I Could Find Them* (Houghton Mifflin Harcourt):
    "Why I Listen to My Children Breathe"

Blue Mesa Review: "Sovereignty"

Superstition Review: "Benevolence"

War, Literature & the Arts: "What My Dead Wife Should Know"

CutBank: "Ishi Wilderness"

Hot Metal Bridge: "Not an Emergency"

Epoch: "The Price of Everything"

Anchor & Knife

The first time I met you I fought your father in the driveway. He fisted a tire iron, but he'd been drinking and he
only clipped my forearm with his looping swing. That's
really where my scar comes from. The afternoon had been
nice, your mother made kabobs, but you wouldn't touch
the green peppers, and you wouldn't speak to me, so your
mom brought the soccer ball out and we kicked at it in
the small backyard and I pretended to know something
about Pelé, and she made you hug me before I left out
the front door, running into your dad, who had spied our
embrace.

You're ten. You stood in front of our autumn oak, your
white-casted right arm at your side above the rocky ground
that shattered your elbow on your fall from the old tree.
I warned you about climbing the dead branches, and still I
ran to you when I heard your animal groan, your dangling
lower arm, inverted, twisting, and I waited to take you to
the hospital and belted you first because you never listened

to me, a stepfather, and it felt good to whip that leather at your lower back, to hear sharpness in the air, and see your body quiet and stiffen.

Sometimes you'd crawl into our bed and curl into your mother. You looked just like her, and I'd imagine you seeping back into her womb, breathing her liquid, splitting into cells, into her egg, his sperm, but when I'd slip into half sleep I'd feel your fingers on my anchor-and-knife tattoo, tracing the shapes.

You tried me two times when you were sixteen, and each time I let you get the first jab in, just so you thought you had a chance. I remember the living room: the worn gray carpet, little bay window; I remember choosing where to land the next blow, then wrestling you down to the floor, lying on top of you, your mother pulling, yelping, pleading as I took your arms above your head and locked them with one of my hands, feeling your helpless slither underneath me, knowing none of it mattered because you weren't mine.

You're twenty. You lifted your sleeve at the dinner table, unveiling your mother's name on your bicep after your first tour in Iraq. When she asked you if you'd killed anyone, your mouth was full of mashed potatoes and you said *I'd go back*. And when you volunteered to go your mother refused to see you off, but I was there, standing and cursing you in the midday heat, watching the C-17 take you away, staying until they began folding up the plastic chairs.

When you called before the battle at al-Qai'm you asked for your mother, and she sobbed and shoved the phone at me, so I took it, and you told me you loved me. You thanked me for the fishing trips on the Truckee River, for sitting in the stands at miserable band performances, for toughening you up for the Marines. And after the battle you told me you'd lied, that you didn't love me, that my belt and fist still filled your dreams, and fearing death had made you say things you thought God wanted to hear.

Your mother and I were pulling weeds in the front yard when the chaplain's clean blue sedan edged up to the curb. He asked us to step inside, but your mother wouldn't budge; she took the news on the sidewalk with a fistful of crabgrass. I drove through a lightning storm to the green bridge we used to fish below. It's where I taught you to smack trout heads against the large black rocks before slicing the guts out.

Once, we tried to catch them with our hands, and I showed you how to reach into the water and rub their soft bellies, lulling them for a moment before the surprise clench and lift. I told you I'd caught hundreds of trout this way, and that my scar was from wrestling a twenty-pounder on the rocks. For all I could tell you believed me.

Your mother fell apart. She locked herself in our darkened bedroom, taking small meals there. She didn't talk to anyone, but on the third day she came to me: *Tell his father*, she said. I waited a couple of hours, and after cursing and circling town, I drove to his place by the lumber mill. My hand gripped the car door handle, but I couldn't pull the damn thing, and I sat there for twenty minutes, his dog barking the whole time. Finally, your father emerged and slowly approached my rusting Ford. He carried a baseball bat in his strong hand. I didn't fancy up the news. *He's dead*, I said, and drove away. I drove until I ran out of gas on a dirt road out by where we shot at clay pigeons. I walked the eight miles back to town.

When I arrived home, your father's truck rested in our driveway. As I passed the truck I looked inside the cab on the chance that he had just arrived, that maybe he was sitting in the driver's seat, buying time, but it was empty. I walked up the steps you helped me build and stood at the threshold with an overwhelming urge to knock at my own door.

We Drag Our Feet
near the Stingrays

I was AWOL going on three days and dad and I were sticking to the crappy highways north of Sacramento when he told me the difference between fucking and making love was where you put your feet. We had stopped at a Burger King in Susanville and both of us fisted double Whoppers. I guess he was trying to help ease my nerves because I hadn't asked a question, and my right leg continued its newfound bounce under the table. I nodded, but didn't laugh, and when he took a bite, I did as well. There was too much mayo on the burger, and I could taste onions I hadn't ordered, but dad was paying, so I kept my mouth shut. I hadn't slept in thirty hours and some damn boy band played from hidden speakers somewhere above us. I wanted to disappear, and dad had a friend that would put me up in Ravendale. We weren't far.

"Feet on the floor," he said, "Making love." A burger bite and swallow. "In a bathtub of Vaseline. Fucking."

"What about a tub of Jell-O?" I said.

"Red or Grape?"

"It matters?" I said.

"Grape seems classier, doesn't it?"

My first laugh in days, but a glance at my black boots shattered my grape Jell-O vision and threw me under the weight of the questions that had pressed me for weeks— *How long would the Army search for me? If they found me, how long in Leavenworth?*

Never in my life had I felt a sense of self-importance, but there in that Burger King, onions on my breath, I imagined black helicopters spotlighting north state backyards, cops everywhere 10-4ing my name back to dispatch.

"Grape is classier," he said, answering his own question. He finished his fries and stood. I hadn't noticed it before, but his jeans seemed new.

"Hitting the head," he said. "Don't run down Main Street."

"You read my mind."

"Get a shake if you want one."

He smiled, but I knew what he meant: "*It's going to be a while before you get another chance.*"

Jesus, he was amazing those first days. He acted like there was nothing amiss in the world. A baker for decades, he still possessed an unshakable optimism about the world even after his millionth glazed donut, even after mom left for Mexico two weeks after she bought me my first bra. He stood in our small kitchen when I came out at sixteen and didn't grimace, just hugged me after a few seconds of open-mouth breathing. And the next morning, he made me eggs for breakfast and said, "At least I don't have to worry about you getting pregnant."

Not that everything was perfect. I remember his fist to my stomach the day he found weed in my sock drawer. And his girlfriends, a new local sleaze every six months, always shacking up with us, eating our food, wrecking our

Corolla. But when I took Claudia to prom dad snapped front yard pictures with pride, even rented us a rundown limo. When I came home one day my senior year and told him I was getting out of Ukiah, that I'd do what mom had done and join the Army and save up for college, he asked me to wait a month, and if I still wanted to join, he'd go with me to sign the papers, so he did. I knew there were wars on, but I thought there was no way in hell they could last much longer, not with the government screwing everything up. And two years later, when I called him and told him I had orders to Iraq, and that as far as I was concerned the Army could go fuck themselves, he asked me what I wanted to do, and when I told him he said "fine," just to give him three days. He picked me up outside Fort Irwin on a Tuesday. First thing he did was run over my cell phone.

I decided on a vanilla shake, and after I ordered and paid with cash the guy working the register asked if my name was Ellie. He swore that he had met me at a party in Tahoe six months prior. I pretended not to be freaked out by pinching my T-shirt then putting my hands in my pockets and staring at his nametag—*Adrian*. He was short and had one vertical line buzzed into each of his eyebrows.

Even though my name isn't Ellie—never was Ellie— and it had been years since my last trip to Tahoe, something told me he was right, that maybe he knew me, or maybe he had been looking for me.

He placed the shake on the counter and put a lid on it. I scanned the corners for cameras, but all I saw were the little holes for the speakers, some John Mayer crap killing us.

I tried not to think of Leavenworth, so I did. The whole sequence in fast forward: Adrian calling me in, a cop in our rear view a few miles out of Susanville, a yellow prison jumper, some cramped cell in nowhere Kansas.

"In South Lake?" he asked.

I shook my head.

"You sure? At Harrah's or something?"

My hands dug in my pockets.

"Tahoe?" he asked.

I shook my head.

"Karen?"

"Please," I said, and grabbed the shake.

"Erin?"

I walked out the doors and leaned on the Corolla. There was smoke in the air. My sunglasses were locked in the car, and I closed my eyes. You can be anywhere with your eyes closed, but I knew I was in Susanville. *Adrian. Leavenworth. A new name?* A diesel downshifted hard on the main drag. Specks of light through my eyelids. The locks popped in the car. Dad's Brut aftershave. I waited for his voice with my eyes closed, but he didn't say anything. I tried to remember what his voice sounded like, but it was hopeless until he said, "Don't tell me, chocolate?"

—z—

I sucked at the shake as we headed east doing just more the speed limit. The tops of mountains burned to the south. It was gorgeous. Fire trucks and cops zoomed by, clueless. Dad pushed the button for recycled air.

"I got a huge buck over there when you were little," he said, pointing at the mountains. "Too bad."

But the fires didn't bother me. I loved that there was so much for everyone to worry about. The market in free fall. Forever war. Illegals everywhere. Fire engulfing the mountains. Homes going up. Probably a desperate guy or two out on their decks armed with garden hoses. They didn't want to die, and that made us the same. I wasn't going to Iraq and coming home messed up. I wasn't willing to stub my goddamned toe over there.

"Thing fed us for a year," he said. "I think that was the time I brought you back an electric pencil sharpener. I always brought you back something. You remember?"

I remembered, but I didn't say anything.

"Some of the best hunting is up by Ravendale," he said. "It's hard to get a tag."

I watched the smoke billow into the sky, flashes of orange flame scattered along the horizon. The hum of the tires on Highway 395. The vanilla shake working its way into my stomach. Dad gave up and put on some Garth Brooks, and neither of us sang along to "The Thunder Rolls."

Right then, I guess I should have been thinking about the rest of my life—how long I'd have to hide, what lies I needed to practice, what I was going to do for money, or a million other things I'd need to figure out in order to stay out of jail. Maybe I should have been thinking about how much my dad loved me, and why he so easily agreed to help. None of that came to me. I was tired, and I thought of my mom, just like I always did right before sleep, and I saw her again in those recurring visions, first with that damn white bra in her hands, holding it out to me in a T.J. Maxx, and then, just her knees down, tan and smooth, her feet in white sand.

<hr />

I awoke by a tree full of shoes.

High desert everywhere. The western edge of the Great Basin. Rocky hills in the distance. This crazy ass tree. Hundreds of shoes dangled from the branches.

Dad talked to a man and a woman under the tree, all of them smiling. The couple didn't look much older than me, and I wondered how dad knew people so young.

I grabbed the door handle and pulled it, but didn't shoulder the door. *What had dad told them?* I blinked the sleep away and watched. The man, shaved clean with a blue Nevada Wolfpack baseball cap. The woman was sleeveless, tan, tall. When she laughed and clapped her hands her triceps flexed. A Chevy pickup a few years old with two boxers in the bed. The wind blew hard enough to move the shoes in the tree, and I wondered if this was what disappearing looked like.

I grabbed my knees like I always do when I'm nervous then opened the door. On the short walk over I kept my eyes on them. Their smiles scared me.

"There she is," dad said.

"Hey," I said. "Thanks for this."

I attempted a little wave, but halfway through it I brought my hand up and brushed back my hair over my right ear.

"Meet Mike and Reggie Miller."

Mike must have seen my nervous grin because he nodded and said, "Yes, like the basketball players."

"What?" dad said.

"NBA," I said.

"Tom, you've never heard of Reggie Miller?" Reggie said. She reached out and touched dad's arm. Her fingernails were painted blue.

"Nope."

"The other Reggie Miller? One of the best shooters of all time?"

"I know Michael Jordan," he said, and frowned.

"That's one," Mike said. "Mike Miller is still playing."

"Grizzlies, right?" I said, and forced eye contact with him, but he looked down. He had a small, c-shaped scar on his left cheek.

"Not sure. We went off satellite last year, so I'm a little out of it."

"OK," I said, because I didn't know what to say. The basketball talk calmed me, but not enough.

"Yeah," Reggie said. "We're radio now. I told him to get rid of the satellite, so he did. There's enough on radio."

A gust of wind and the dull sound of shoes knocking. I looked up at the shoes, but I didn't recognize any of them.

"Sure."

"We get the stations out of Reno mainly," she said. She clapped her hands then hushed the boxers even though they weren't barking. "Point is, you're welcome to stay with us if you want to."

"There's no choice," dad said. "Courtney knows."

"I'm not forcing her to do anything," Reggie said, pointing at me. "She only comes if she wants to."

"You agreed," dad said.

"Who you talking to?" Reggie said.

"It's fine," I said. "Yes. I mean. Of course, I'll go."

Just then dad took three quick steps toward the Corolla then stopped. He kicked the ground and stared back at us, the color out of this face.

"We're talking too long," he said. "We should've met someplace else. This damn tree." He pressed his hands together. "What are we doing? Come on, basketball? Radio?"

"Easy, dad."

"Grab your stuff," he said. "Now."

"No one's out here, Tom," Reggie said. She opened her arms out wide.

"Now," he said. "We made it all the way here. No one knows what the hell is going on, and we're talking about the fucking basketball teams."

He was right, but I didn't know it then.

"Jesus," I said, and dug my fingernails into my hands.

"You called me and now I've done this," he said. "Get your things."

I did, and he hugged me hard. He kissed the top of my head then he squeezed my shoulders and gave me a push. I went back on my heels and I looked at him to see the surprise in his face, but there was none.

He'd saved me, but it didn't feel like it, not then. He wanted me gone.

I guess I should have thanked him, but for some reason I showed him my palms and said, "Fine. Go."

We watched him leave, and Mike grabbed my stuff and loaded the two bags into the truck. I stood by the tree for a minute trying to get my legs underneath me. The sky above us was clear, but to the south I could see the smoke haze in the distance. Reggie gave me a few seconds then walked over.

"Those red ones are mine," she said, pointing at a pair of little kid's shoes on a branch about ten feet up. Unlike the other shoes, hers seemed new, or at least barely worn. When I looked closer I saw the small Nike swooshes. I thought about asking if they were her son's shoes, but I stopped myself. I watched the shoes twist in the tree and waited, and when she turned and walked away I followed her.

Early on with the Millers I sat on the back steps in the morning and stared out at the desert. Sometimes I heard sirens in the wind. I thought about dad sometimes, working the donuts to life. Often I wondered who was getting blown up in Iraq, and if I knew them. Sometimes I wondered if the person that went in my place was getting blown up. I tried to convince myself that I didn't care. I stomped my feet on the steps. I dug my fingers into my quads and felt the pressure, my whole body connected.

If I learned anything in those early days it was that all of the philosophizing about returning to nature and finding yourself in nature and loving nature and mother earth, all of that shit, was wrong. At least it was a few miles east of Ravendale on County Road 503.

There was wind and deserted dirt roads. Empty skies and sagebrush and brown rock and summer snakes. Salt licks out back and Mike gunning down deer and antelope from the back steps. There was me with my hands in the warm, dead bodies of animals pulling out the gray guts and skinning off their hides.

I had my hands in the slick guts. I yanked on the intestines and smelled the stench, and I wasn't upset, but I thought about what I wanted to be. I was twenty. I was always cold. I pulled out a stomach or lungs and plopped them onto the ground, and I remembered sitting in class in Ukiah and wondering if I'd be a good teacher. I still thought about that, if I could teach reading or math, if I'd be any good, but I knew there was a background check if you wanted to be a teacher. Still, I let myself give into the daydreams out there in the brush for a few moments, but it never lasted long. The guts steamed in the morning and I looked at my hands and knew—*This is what I am.*

⌐

Eight months after the shoe tree handoff, I walked into the house to loud classical music. I'd found the lost goat and gathered eggs for breakfast, so my hands were dirty and full. A couple days prior I mentioned something about missing great music. I didn't specify.

Reggie stood in the living room next to the old Pioneer speakers, Mike in the kitchen in swim trunks. They were proud.

"Fuck Beethoven," I said.

I had no idea if it was Beethoven, but eloquence and obscenity melted their brains. I smiled to let them know I was joking, but Mike went into the bedroom and shut the door.

"Courtney," Reggie said.

I cracked the eggs into the pan, and I let Reggie rub my back. She'd kissed me once, but I wasn't interested then. Her hand felt good on me.

"Here's something," she said. "I've never known anyone who has died."

"No."

"Seriously."

"You've got to turn down that music," I said.

"I've heard of people dying, of course, but everyone close to me, all alive."

She stopped rubbing me, and I wondered if she remembered that she'd shown me the red Nikes. Even if she did, what was there to say?

"Are you happy for me?"

"Sure," I said. "Am I going to live forever?"

"Not one person."

"Amazing."

"I'm not stupid," she said. "I know it's coming, only that I haven't had to deal with any of that. I've never been to a funeral."

"Turn the damn music down."

"Are you listening to me?"

"Yes," I said.

"What I'm saying is how can I know what I want if no one I know has died?"

I turned to face her. She had been kind to me, but she angered easily.

"Don't wish for it," I said.

Mike opened the bedroom door.

"Stay in there," Reggie said, and he closed the door.

"We should go for a drive," she said. "He's been pissing me off. Giving the dogs the wrong food and all that hell."

"I'm making eggs."

"You think I don't want to be here, right?" she said. "Go on with your eggs."

I turned back around and fumbled with the spatula. She put her hand on my back.

"Who knows?" she said. "It's better than Reno I guess. Just whores running around."

I turned the burner off.

"Have you seen these whores?"

"What do you want?" she said. "I mean, where do you want to go?"

A simple question, but one I didn't have an answer to. I hadn't let myself think that far ahead although I had plenty of time to come up with a plan, or at least a wish. I knew dreams were dangerous. I kept my back to her.

"You don't know?" she said.

I laughed, and the sound devastated me.

"Everyone says 'somewhere warm,'" she said. "That doesn't sound smart to me."

"Iraq is warm."

"Are we joking about that now?" she said.

"Why not."

"Iraq as vacation spot? Tourism probably isn't booming."

"Only one way to get there," I said.

"What's that?"

"Enlist."

—

No cell service, no internet, no television. Just the radio with three reliable stations: country, old country-western, and some pirate station that tried to convince us that the world would end at any minute. But the few times I went into Alturas I knew the world was still alive, and probably would remain so for a while. We once ate at The Black Bear Diner, and when the waitress called me "Honey" I fought the desperate pangs of belonging. Besides her, no one looked at me. Not in Alturas or Likely or Termo. And when I checked, nothing in the paper mentioned *any* missing person.

—

No one, anywhere, was thinking about me. Not dad, who hadn't visited in six months. Not the Army, who I assumed by that point had better things to worry about. Not even the locals, who must have bought the lie that I was Mike's cousin.

When the fighter jets from Klamath buzzed the hills, my nerves no longer flared up. I laughed when the jackass on the radio stuttered out that the government had us all under surveillance. Even so, I wasn't begging to run into the Sheriff or anyone else. I knew how to milk goats and fix a fence. I could tell the difference between a crow, a raven, and a buzzard. None of it mattered, but I was alive.

There were enough good days—the hours after an afternoon thundershower would soften the land. The few times a year herds of rabbits would swarm the hills around us like some harmless apocalypse. The day Mike taught me how to waltz to the horrible classical music CD he'd bought for me. The second time Reggie kissed me.

It wasn't inevitable. We were in the garage. She was holding a gallon of milk in each hand. I thanked her for cleaning my room and she kissed me on the cheek then she went inside.

Mike and Reggie teased me about my hatred of Dolly Parton, my aversion to olives, and the fact that I owned four San Francisco Giants T-shirts, and I gave it back to them about everything from their diet (meat and more meat) to their décor. The living room walls were decorated with pictures that changed by the season. Spring—Elvis; Summer—Aztec, New Mexico; Autumn—Deer and Elk; Winter—US Presidents. My favorite was a picture of a white sign, black lettering, "Welcome to Aztec. 6378 Friendly People & 6 Old Soreheads," that hung from June through August by the fireplace.

In their bedroom they had a dozen photographs of their nephews and nieces. They rarely talked about them, but one day I found a pregnancy test on the living room sofa and Reggie told me they were trying to start a family. It was the only time I saw her cry, and even then, it was only tears. No hysterics or heaving or gasps. I held her and she put her feet on my feet. It hurt, but I didn't say anything. Her head was on my shoulder, and I looked around the room at photos of Aztec as she repeated, "Just one."

—

It's true, I'd been granted my wish. I wasn't in Iraq. I rarely thought of IEDs or sniper fire. I had all my limbs. No traumatic brain shit. In the mornings out on the back steps, I no longer wondered about the person that went in my place. We all make choices.

But I did think about the day outside Fort Irwin, how easy it was to get into the Corolla, and if all of this was still a crime. What would I say in front of a judge? *I just wanted to live.* Could that be enough? *I wasn't willing to die there.* What if everyone agreed that the war was a mistake? If that was true, and it seemed to be true, then didn't I make the right decision?

—

We were all in bed—me, Reggie, and Mike. Mike was sleeping. He was a good listener and he followed the rules. He could touch me above the waist, but no erections. An erection and I was out of there, back to my room. If he asked me to touch him I was out of there. It wasn't about him, and he understood.

Earlier that night he sat on the edge of the bed with a belt around his neck like we told him to. He never said anything.

Mike started snoring and Reggie kicked him. She'd had coffee with dinner, and I knew she'd be up late.

Her head rested on my stomach and I knew her mind was spinning by the way she clicked her tongue.

"Why can't we get the truth?" she said. "The oil spill in the Gulf of Mexico, all of these jerks saying that it's a catastrophe. Said the same thing about the Exxon spill in Alaska. No one's talking about that one anymore. Same thing here. Wait five years and it will be forgotten. But now, the world is ending. Every day on the radio, 'It's destroyed forever!' The world is ending. Over oil? So a few thousand birds die, and this is the world event we care about? What the hell are we doing? And we cry and cry over these things, but like two million people die of starvation every year, and we're worried about damn birds?"

She'd started using a new conditioner and my fingers glided through her hair.

"Preach," I said.

"Don't say that. I'm not preaching."

"Fine. What else?"

She was quiet for a while, and I could hear Mike's breathing. He slept the best of all of us.

"You know the gay guy in Wyoming that was killed all those years ago? Found him out by a fence. And the whole damn country was up in arms because it's a hate crime. Rednecks in Wyoming should go to hell and everything. Dead guy becomes the poster child for all the discrimination in the world. He was a saint. Never did anything wrong. Poor little man just liked other guys, so he gets a play in his honor. Rallies and donations. And you know what? Turns out that his murder had nothing to do with him being gay. Guy was a filthy drug dealer. Guy screwed with the wrong people. Got killed because he was a druggy asshole. But does the media tell us that? Is there a play about that? Pisses me off."

"No one knows anything," I said.

"You don't believe that."

"What do you think I'm doing here?"

She lifted her head and kissed my ribs.

"You're here because you're strong. That's it."

"That's it?"

"Tell me you're strong. Say it."

"Motivational speaker?" I said.

"I know you."

"Keep guessing."

"You've seen someone killed, right?"

"What?"

"I know you have. Tell me."

"Psycho," I said.

"Tell me. Story time."

"It's not that interesting."

"Death?"

"I didn't even see the guy," I said.

"Confess."

"It's not a confession, but my prom night I saw a motorcycle get hit."

"A motorcyclist you mean."

"Orr Springs Road, outside my hometown. We'd been up in the hills. On the drive back the van in front of us went over the double yellow and hit the bike, but we kept on driving."

"Damn," she said.

"We were so messed up. We got back to her house and we didn't know what to do so we took some ecstasy and put on *The Wizard of Oz*."

"Prom night?"

"Yeah," I said. "We were crying. We thought we were screwed, that the cops would be showing up to the doorstep. But we kept our mouths shut, and no one ever showed."

"See. Strong."

She kissed my ribs again then crawled over me to Mike and held him. I was sweating.

"I love him," she said, although I'd never asked her to prove it.

"He's never been sick, okay?" she said.

"Okay."

I put my hand on her back and felt her heart going like crazy.

"Never," she said. "And there's a guy named Ray Kurzweil, he's never been sick either. Some genius, and he's taking pills that will keep him alive forever. Don't laugh. I'm serious. Like a hundred pills a day. He's so damn smart and he created the first program that types what you say into it. Not that that has to do with anything, only that he's created all this stuff, invented everything, and he's trying to live forever. But his biggest project is he's trying to bring his father back to life."

"Stop," I said.

"Listen to me. It's true. He's invented all this stuff. People call him Frankenstein. I'm sure he gets laughed at, but he is, no shit, smart enough to bring his father back to life. He's trying at least."

"Good for him."

"He knows what he wants because he knows someone that died."

"Again, Reggie?"

"Listen, Mike's never been sick."

"Okay, I believe you," I said.

"I'm saying that Kurzweil knows what he wants. He could have anything, but he wants his dad."

"You mean you want what you can't have?"

"No," she said. "I mean he wants his dad. Have you been listening?"

"Where's your dad?"

I said it before I thought about saying it, but I wanted to know.

I kept my hand on her back and felt her heartbeat. It was the same fast beating, but she was quiet. All I knew about her childhood was that she was from Carson City, that she'd had a pig named Oreo, and that she'd done a year at Truckee Meadows Community College.

Reggie reached back for me and I gave her my hand.

"He's not dead," she said.

—~—

One day there was an Amber Alert on the country station. A boy had been abducted on the way to school in Sparks. The public was asked to be on the lookout for a red Dodge Dakota, Nevada plates. The boy's mother came on and destroyed us with her pleas. I thought of her pain, about how easy it was to kidnap, about all of the red Dakotas that were innocent. Later, I heard that the boy was found out at Pyramid Lake, alive and untouched, with his *Star Wars* backpack. I couldn't make sense of it then and still can't, except that maybe there's no justice in the world.

—⁓—

Every Tuesday on the pirate radio station a woman would come on and read for an hour. Everything from Harry Potter to Montaigne to Robert Service. I'd sit on the carpet and listen contently, but then she would sign off with "Remember, freedom is the only thing that matters." That always pissed me off. Why ruin a great book with that crap.

Ask anyone what freedom means and they'll look at you funny then say something about liberty. But when you ask them about liberty they'll look at you funny then say something about privacy. Press them about privacy and they'll say something about freedom. Everyone claims they want to be left alone, but I don't buy it.

—⁓—

Dad drew an X5a hunting tag in October of 2011, so I met him at 4 a.m. out on Grasshopper Road west of Termo. I knew something was wrong when he pulled up in a new Ford F-150. He brought his latest sleaze, Marci, who wore pink boots and had hair down to her ass. I was furious, but I let her talk.

Within two minutes I knew everything: she'd won $400,000 off a scratcher lottery ticket a few months prior. The truck was a present for dad. She'd invited him to move in.

"I know it's a lot to take in," dad said, but Marci interrupted him.

"And I can keep quiet about you," she said.

"Can you?" I said.

"Yes," she said, and reached for dad's hand.

"Perfect," I said.

"They've stopped calling," dad said. "I'm not saying it's over. But it used to be every month I'd get a call. They're still probably looking at my call history. I'm not sure."

"They're not looking at your calls," Marci said. "You know how many people have run off? Thousands and thousands."

"I don't know," dad said.

I shook my head.

"Sure," Marci said. "Thousands. But there's no recruiting problem, so they pretty much let you go."

"Marci," I said. "You don't know what's happening."

"Obama's ending the war," she said. "I know that much. For all the other shit he's up to, at least he's doing that."

"Okay," dad said. "Enough of that. We're all here now."

I didn't know what that meant, and just as my frustration rushed at me Marci handed me a coffee.

"Your dad says you like a ton of sugar. Me, too."

That bought my silence for a few minutes as I tried to figure out how I'd get some time with dad.

We headed south until Pine Creek and stopped and unloaded. Brutally cold outside, dad offered me his old .243 rifle for mountain lions, but I had brought Mike's .40 sig, so I waved him off. Within two minutes Marci had decided to stay in the truck.

Dad and I set up two ridges over from the truck overlooking a long draw. The sun came up on our backs, and we stayed quiet for a long time. The light did nothing to the cold, and I watched my breath push out from my mouth. My feet and hands ached. Dad sat close to me, but I couldn't smell him.

"Nothing here," dad whispered. "Head back?"

"Can we take out Marci?"

Dad smirked and stood, then gathered kindling and started a fire. My hands hurt as they warmed.

"You've been out there long enough, I guess," dad said.

"You guess?"

"I don't know how to help," he said. "That's what I'm trying to say."

I didn't have an immediate answer, and I wasn't going to pretend. I'd forgiven him for our initial goodbye long before. What else was he supposed to do? No one knew my plans because there weren't any, and I didn't know then what help I needed. The smoke shifted at me and I edged to my right.

"What are you doing with her?" I said.

"I don't ask what you're doing. I only ask if you need help. You make your choices."

"Ask me," I said. "What do you want to know?"

"What do you want me to say?"

"Jesus," I said. "Fine."

"That I should have taken you somewhere else? How was I to know?"

"Know what?" I said.

He didn't say anything, and I pressed him with "Tell me," but only once. He stared into the fire and shook his head. I looked down at the draw and didn't see anything.

From somewhere in the distance a guttural, manufactured sound. It stopped then came again.

"What the hell?" I said.

"Honking," he said. "That's my truck's horn."

"Wow, Marci's a keeper."

"She's fine."

I stood, but he didn't move.

"She can wait."

"What?"

"When you were a kid, you always…"

"Shit, dad. Just stop."

"What do you want, then?" he said. "Why are you out here?"

"You asked me, remember? It's that easy."

"You act like we have to learn something every time we're together," he said. "I just wanted to see you. That's enough."

"You've seen me once. Are you serious?"

He took off his gloves and held his hands to the fire, and his hands were wrong, clawed, the middle, ring, and pinkie fingers curled in tight to his palm. I watched for a moment waiting for him to open his hands.

"What are you doing?" I said. "Your hands. Jesus, dad."

"Viking disease," he said.

"What the hell are you talking about?"

"That's what they call it, Viking disease."

"You can't move them?" I said. "You can't. They're stuck like that?"

"It's not serious. I can have surgery. It came on quick. I spent years in the bakery."

"Spent?" I said. "You're not baking?"

"Are you serious? Look at my hands. I haven't worked for a year."

"What?"

"Almost two years."

I stared at his hands, like play guns. He held them to the fire.

"What are you doing for money? I mean…," but I cut off as soon as I pictured Marci.

Dad looked at the fire, and I don't know what I expected from him in that moment. Defeat? Pain?

"I'm fine," he said. "I'm here."

"You can have surgery."

But he was off somewhere else. His eyes on my feet.

"When you were a kid you always asked to come hunting with me. And I always said no, but you'd always want me to bring something back."

"I know this story," I said. "The electric pencil sharpener. And look now, we're hunting! Stop. Your hands."

"No. Let me finish. You'd want something when I got back. Not just the damn pencil sharpener. But always I'd give you something. A Hot Wheel or some stickers."

He paused then scratched his face.

"Yeah. So?"

"I didn't buy them. I mean, I gave them to you, but your mom bought them in Ukiah. She'd have them ready when I got home, and then I'd give them to you."

"What are you saying? So you didn't give me the shitty stickers, who cares?"

"I don't know," he said. "It bothers me that you think that I got them when I didn't."

"That's what bothers you? What are you trying to do, give mom some credit?"

"No, this is about me and you. I want your memories to be right."

"Are you serious?"

The horn sounded again and dad stood.

"I'm serious," he said.

He didn't hug me or pat me on the back, and when we started walking he said, "We'll keep this between us," but I had no idea what he meant.

We walked together up and down the two ridges. It was quiet, expect for our boots on the ground. I had no idea that it would be the last time I'd have with him alone. Even if I did, I don't know what I would have changed. Maybe I would have asked him to stay out there with me a little longer. Maybe I did want to talk about mom.

As soon as we got within sight of the truck he stopped and said, "Brace yourself. I know she's a lot to take." He could always make me laugh, and that's something.

When we got back to the truck Marci opened the door and said, "Nothing?"

⁓

Later that evening, after dad and Marci left, I sat in Mike's truck alone up near Observation Peak. Mike had given me a little weed and I smoked as the sun went down.

I kept the window down as a courtesy even though it was cold. I was still trying to escape the new car smell of dad's truck, Marci's pink boots. I imagined what I would get if I won $400,000 in the lottery, but the beach house–Ferrari dream faded as soon as I realized there was probably a background check involved, or at least publicity of one sort or another.

I couldn't see a single person or home in the basin below me. The view and the weed calmed me. Life wasn't hard for me then, but I understood nothing in my future would be easy. I wouldn't be able to stay out there forever. I knew that, but each day passed and everything seemed more comfortable—the Chevy, sagebrush, night noises, living room pictures, their touch.

I didn't love Reggie or Mike and they didn't love me, at least in the way that would keep me in their home. Affection isn't love.

I sat in the driver's seat and watched the valley go dark.
I wasn't trying to force my mind anywhere, so it wandered.
*My dad's hands. The shoe tree. Swimming lessons when I was
eight. Signing my name at the recruiter's office. The woman's
voice reading Robert Service. An iPod Christmas present.
Watching mom undress. Finding that goat near the dry ditch.* I
couldn't make sense of it then, but now, I think that's what
it means to know yourself, that you remember enough
about your life that you know who to be.

It was dark when I rolled up the window. I was tired
but relaxed as I drove down the dirt road. I would sleep
well.

About a mile before the 503 I saw the rabbits. There was
a herd of them in my headlights, a thousand maybe, more
than I'd ever seen. They huddled together in my lights.
Brown like the dirt. Pathetic and helpless.

I wasn't angry when I pressed the gas. I was strong. I
knew that. It had been so long since I felt invincible, but
I felt it out on that dirt road in the Chevy. The smallest
bumps under the truck, like driving over a stretch of wash-
board. No blood or guts. Just the harmless rattle of the
truck. My keys bouncing into the steering column. The
smallest shake of my hands, and I knew that nothing could
happen to me. I would never be hurt. No one could tell me
no. It was an easy choice. Not even a choice, just a silent
move with my foot.

―――

One day in Alturas I saw a couple of vets at the pizza place.
Reggie and I were there on a Sunday watching the Niners
destroy the Rams, minding our business in the far corner.
I overheard one guy telling the bartender that he'd been in
for eight years and hadn't deployed once. His friend said

that he saw time in Iraq and Afghanistan. It was stupid, but I imagined that this was the guy that took my place. I ignored the game for a while and watched him. When the Rams scored he cursed quietly. He talked about the small fire out by Devil's Garden, about cattle near Canby. He scratched his ear a lot. When they walked out of the place in the middle of the fourth quarter, neither of them limped or grimaced or cursed their place in the world. Is it wrong to say I was surprised? That I was expecting some outward proof, at least from the one? I must have been staring because Reggie tapped my arm and asked me what I was looking at. I said "Nothing," which was true.

Mike kissed my collarbone. I'd given him permission a few weeks before, but he'd waited, and I could hear the ecstasy in his short breaths. We had all the lights on in the house, and I sat on the kitchen counter with my jeans on. Earlier that evening we had a fight about how much longer I was going to stay, and I thought we had settled on another three months. Mike and Reggie wanted to adopt a child. I didn't blame them.

Mike kissed me, and I waited for Reggie to come over and tell Mike to go away, but she said, "I'm calling the Sheriff tomorrow. I won't call if you're gone by lunch."

—

Who do I want to be? I want to be alive.

I lived in Ravendale. I've been on a Greyhound at 2 a.m. in West Texas. I worked the docks outside Memphis. I've picked up trash in a VA hospital.

Freedom? Please. I've seen the misshapen heads of vets with traumatic brain injuries. I've seen their kids crawl on them as they moan. I've seen a dead woman floating in the

Mississippi. I've seen little red Nikes in the shoe tree. I've seen a boy step in front of a train then change his mind at the last second. Wanting to be alive is the only thing that matters.

On St. George Island there are a couple family-run restaurants, a lighthouse, and enough vacation homes to keep the restaurants open. In the morning you can see the shrimp boats in the shallows between the island and the Florida mainland.

After work I take my daughter to the beach. No one knows us because everyone there is a visitor looking out on the gulf waiting for a dolphin to crest or a red sunset. They look out at the gulf and can't imagine anything bad ever happening out there. I don't blame them, but I don't believe in forgetting.

In autumn we all have to watch out for the stingrays. They come in close to shore, thousands of them. You can see them everywhere. The warning signs say that you only get stung if you step on one, so we drag our feet on the sandy bottom.

Feed

I'm going to feed you, I know you don't want me to, but I'm
going to feed you, I'm going to push this tube down your
nose, down into your stomach, and I'm not going to lube
it up because I want this whole thing to go slow, I want
you to feel me at work, and I see you there shackled to
the chair, I saw you squirming before I came in the room,
I watched you through the little window in the door, you
were twitching and sweating, trying to convince yourself
that you were somewhere else, maybe back in your cell,
maybe back home, and when I walked in I could tell you
liked me right away, a woman, you thought, easier, and I
saw you relax because you were worried it might be some
rough-and-tumble blockhead Marine, but no, you got me,
and you think I'm going to go easy on you, you're guessing
I don't want to be in Cuba either, these shitty hot summer days, but you're wrong, I want to be here with you at
Guantanamo, I want to be the one that keeps you alive,
I want to be the one that forces food down into you, I
want to prolong your life, and two minutes ago you had

an empty room, you had fading hope that you'd starve to death, gorgeous martyrdom, but now you have me, and I'm going to give you this minute, I'll let you think that you have a woman who is going to take it easy on you, a weak woman here to comfort you, to talk to you when I thread that pipe down your nose, maybe you think I'll whisper to you like your mother used to do, maybe I'll tell you it's going to be okay or that it will be over in a minute, but that's not what you're going to get, you're getting a dry tube shoved down into your stomach, and you're going to gag and beg me to stop but you won't be able to speak, you'll only give me a whine and a gurgle, and I'll ignore you, and you're shackled tight and I'm going to show you this bottle of Ensure so you know that you're getting the good stuff, the shit with all of the calories that will fatten you up for life, and I see you looking me up and down, hello there, it's me, and you don't know it yet, but I'll be here tomorrow and the day after that and the day after that, we'll just hit repeat on this feed, but let's just start with today, right now, and you can watch me pull the cover down on the little window in the door and walk toward you, take another few seconds to breathe deep, feel that stale air enter your body, scan around the room and look at those white cinderblock walls, breathe deep and look back at me, yes, here I am, I'm going to feed you, I know you don't want me to, take this nod and think about what it means, wish for your mother's voice in my throat, take these seconds and breathe, think about your hunger strike, you and your buddies sending a message, yes, good, give me that scowl, go ahead, you want me to know you're a tough guy, but take a moment and think about the days you've gone without food, you and your buddies trying to get our attention, and guess what, we got the message, got it loud and clear, and here I am, ready to fatten you up, I'll keep you alive, yes, you see that bottle, yes, speak to me, chant at me, let's get religious, show me your soul, sing to me, turn it up, good, keep it going as I set up, pray for salvation, sing the devastation of facing more days on this earth, chant at me tough guy, keep it going, good, louder now, yes, I hear you, you want another nod, I know it, here you go, pray at me, close those eyes, sing me back to Carson City and my son, you think that's where I want to be, but know that I can wait, at least a little longer, because I want you to live, already I'm studying your nose, your nostrils, which one I will choose, yes, I'm checking you out, this woman, you think, who will speak to you as your mother did, this Marine, she doesn't want to be here, but I'm here, I chose to be here, to hang this bottle, to puncture it with one end of the tube and ready the other end between my fingertips, and I'll tighten your head restraint first, let me get close to you, think of me and smell me, calm yourself, you'll live, you are here to live, and I'm going to feed you, I'm going to control you, yes, I hold the tube in front of your eyes and you quiet down, yes, this is going into you, take this nod, yes, this will hurt, feel the tip in your left nostril, I'll leave it there for a moment, it tickles, go ahead, feel the tip in you, just barely into you, think about how you'll fight it, how you'll feel the dryness all the way down, how you'll gag and beg and squirm like you're dying, but I'm saving you, prolonging you, this Ensure hanging beside us is your savior, I'm here, I'll keep you alive, feel the tube in your nostril, feel it start down, dry, slow, feel it catch and feel me push harder, yes, let's take our time, feel the plastic enter you, curve into you, yes, try to call out, I'm here, feel the plastic catch on something deep now, I push again and you spasm, yes, groan, louder, yes, that tube deep, and with the other nostril you smell me, smell the soap from my shower, smell my breath from my breakfast, shake those limbs and test the arm shackles, yes, test them again, that pipe sliding down into you, the pain and pressure, yes, and yell out at those cinderblocks, at the summer heat, yes, we're here, and you're ready for the good stuff, the Ensure, white and thick working into you, you fight it, but you're not going anywhere, no one waits for you, and there it is, you feel it in your sinus first, the coolness trickles deep, yes, test those shackles, gasp, go ahead, I'm here, cry it out, you'll live, and I'm the reason, fight it all you want, it's too late, the liquid seeps into your body, healing you, it's me, yes, look at me, right here, take this nod and think about what it means, listen to me, calm down and listen to me, hear my voice as I speak to you, these are the only words you'll get, calm down, listen to me say, "I'm feeding you."

Tendons

Fifteen miles outside the town of Chester, in the far
northern reaches of California, the eighty-person Jefferson Militia bathes in Echo Lake the day before their
planned takeover. Naked and freezing, they pass around
an industrial-sized plastic bottle of Dawn dish soap and
squeeze enough green liquid onto their bodies to give
them hope.

J1, their commander, washes her muscular and scarred
arms. She calls out to me, "We do everything together,
Marcos. You see? You see?"

I snap a couple of shots with my iPhone then start a
video.

"Last Supper shit, but we wash ourselves," she says.

J1 isn't fatalistic, and her Last Supper reference sur-
prises me—Jesus knew what was coming, right?—but the
lathered militia is unfazed or unaware. The lake water is
cold, cold, cold.

Jones, on guard duty, keeps smelling the barrel of his
AR-15. I can't blame him. The gun oil smell intoxicates.

Like everyone else here, he would kill me if he thought it would help the cause.

Jones should probably be facing the other direction—away from the lake, surveying the entry points—but no one comes up here in early April. There's still snow in the shadows.

"This is nothing," J1 says. "This is just the beginning. Just wait. By tomorrow evening, we'll have a thousand with us. The next day, two thousand."

She believes this or just wants to, and maybe she's right, but surely it's a hell of a thing to convince a thousand people a day to join her militia and demand the new state of Jefferson, especially with its shifting agenda and proposed borders—some days it's Sacramento north to the Oregon border, some days it's Chico north—but J1 says those arguments will be settled later. For tomorrow and the early days thereafter, the only thing that matters is the spark, the idea of Jefferson, that it could be a real thing.

The Jefferson Militia's prospects ride on news coverage of their takeover of Chester, population 2,200. J1 bets that all she needs is a few days, a reporter with a functioning camera and microphone, and enough antigovernment locals to help secure the entry points to town. "Humble ingredients," she's told me more than once.

J1 has paid close attention to the Bundy standoff up in Oregon and knows hers isn't a hopeless crusade. Sure, Bundy's was only a wildlife refuge, while hers is a takeover of an actual town, but J1 figures the militia will trend on Twitter and Facebook within 30 minutes of the road blockade—she'll tweet updates herself—and appear on "Breaking News" banners scrolling across the major cable news networks by noon tomorrow.

As for my participation, I've already told her I'm not releasing any footage in real time. I'm a filmmaker, not a reporter. There's a difference.

J1 washes her breasts and I pause the video and lower the phone.

"You stop when I wash my tits, and you got a hundred guys playing with their dicks. Have you learned nothing?"

J1's right, of course.

If Sasha were here, she'd agree. When Sasha was pissed at her Chechen leaders she would rant at me. Her favorite maxim: biology has nothing to do with ingenuity.

"Chivalry is sexist as hell," J1 says. "And discretion is different than chivalry. I wash my body, we wash our bodies, because we believe in being clean. This isn't just about Los Angeles stealing all of our goddamn water."

"Damn right, J1" Jones says.

I learned early only leaders get the letter-number distinction here at Echo Lake. It's easier to remember the chain of command. They did the same thing in Chechnya.

"Start the video," J1 says.

I do.

"How many Americans have actually read our entire Constitution, plus all amendments? What percentage?"

I shrug and keep my 2% guess to myself. The less of recorded me the better. I'll voice over in postproduction if needed.

"What do you think, Jones?" she says.

"Ten percent," he says. "Maybe."

"Point one percent," J1 says.

She lowers herself into the lake, head above water.

"Everyone you see here, each and every one, has read it all. And thought about it. Deeply. We talk about it. Engaged citizenship. And, listen, we're not just some redneck psychos. We're realists. We know there's very little black and white in this world. We know governing is a difficult business. So what? The one thing we won't abide is purposeful ignorance. And that's what's taken over. Celebrated. It's a race to the fucking bottom. The less you know, the more popular you become. Insta-ites. Trump-ites. Everyone related by dumbassery. We've had enough bullshit. That," she smiles and points at Jones, "and Los Angeles stealing our water."

She must be nervous because she's told me all of this before, or she simply forgets I have this type of speech recorded already.

I've witnessed the militia's mandatory constitution discussions, lucid and nuanced for the most part. The 16th Amendment–income tax conversation a few nights ago will certainly make the final cut of the documentary. J1's soliloquy on the progression of social democracy and economics, namedropping Smith, Marx, Keynes, and Friedman alongside Pynchon, Streisand, and Jay-Z, will surely be a highlight. I found it confusing and unknowable, which means it will be celebrated. I already picture the scene on living room big screens across America, J1's late afternoon speech on the lakeshore edited with "99 Problems" thumping through Bose speakers.

J1 reapplies some Dawn on her neck and ears then washes it off.

"Enough of the Know-Nothings and trolls," she says. "And the goddamn sex tape prophets."

I pause the video.

"Why is that important to you?" I say, and immediately regret it. This is a first-day embed question, not a day-before-the-attack question. It sounds weak leaving my mouth. I've been with them for two months and I should know better. This is my first realization that I, too, am nervous about tomorrow.

"Marcos," she says, disappointed, but not angry.

"Scratch that," I say.

Jones stands and shakes his legs out. He holds the AR-15 out to me, but I don't take it. He's been doing this move—trying to get me to hold his weapon—from the first day I arrived. He thinks it's funny. Some days I do, too, but not today.

"You sure?" he says.

"No," I say.

"You're a Jefferson patriot if you hold it or not," he says.

"Not true," I say.

"You can think that," Jones says. "But you're fucking wrong. You haven't called the cops."

"There's another reason you're wrong," J1 says to me. "We're all patriots. Everyone. Everywhere. The sad part is most are status quo patriots. We all want something. That doesn't change. Our group just wants something better, something informed, and we're willing to act."

It pisses me off that they're right, at least the part about specialized human desire, and I can't help but worry I've fallen into a false perception of safety with the militia.

Most people find nothing initially endearing about J1, but the depth of her belief, combined with the power of her knowledge of history and logic, eventually does pull one close. I understand the militia's J1 adulation, but I also know worship often arrives with a sense of false security.

In Mexico and Chechnya there was always planned death to remind me of the stakes. Here, it's yellow "Don't

Tread on Me" flags and speeches about liberty, taxes, and resolve. The violence thus far has been relatively quiet and quick. Among the militia there have been a few fistfights, and once, when a man tried to desert the militia, J1 slit him from hip to knee with a nine-inch blade. Yet death still feels distant, and I'm not sure why. Maybe tomorrow will change everything.

Soon, most of the men and women walk out of the lake and dry off. It's Jones's turn to bathe. He needs it. Before he leaves he tosses me a stick of beef jerky.

"Calories," he says.

"How many people by tomorrow, Jones?" J1 says.

"A thousand," Jones says. "At least. Once they see what we're offering they'll come running."

Jones isn't stupid, and like most of my days with the Jefferson Militia I marvel at the human capacity for aggressive optimism, a not-too-distant cousin of loneliness.

I've seen it elsewhere.

Jones walks away and hands his AR-15 to a newly dressed N3—even leaders pull guard duty. N3 is a five-foot-tall Citadel grad with a Winnie-the-Pooh tattoo on her right forearm. She grabs a foldable chair and sets up next to me. She hates that I'm here, filming and taking photos. From what I've seen the only person she trusts is J1.

"Marcos," N3 says. "Stop that video shit."

I know better than to argue. She once tossed my old phone and notepad into the lake, and threatened to skin me alive, a seemingly genuine threat, so I slide my iPhone into my pocket.

J1 walks out of the lake, dries, and wraps a large UC Santa Cruz towel around her waist. She nears me, fighting the cold.

I've never seen this towel, and I'm about to say "Banana Slugs," when she says "I'd take a hundred people tomorrow. You know that, right? Hell, I'd take fifty. I need all of these people to believe. In the moment, it won't matter if it's fifty or a thousand."

But that's not true, and I'm positive she knows it, too. Or at least she did before this moment. I wonder where she is in her own mind.

She really is a marvel: I've heard her recite the Saint Crispin's Day speech from memory then tell brutal stories of rape and disfigurement from her time in Chowchilla prison. But here, now, after all the preparation and target practice and hope, where is she in her consciousness?

The uncertainty of the next day doesn't haunt all of us equally.

How could it?

"You overthink things," N3 says to me.

Sasha used to tell me the same damn thing, but how could I not overthink when I knew Sasha's mission was to detonate a suicide vest? It was winter when she covered the explosives lining her chest with a purple Adidas coat.

"He's remembering something," J1 says. "Be careful, Marcos, retrospection is one of the worst drugs."

"Answer her," N3 says.

I stare at J1's towel.

"You still digesting my Last Supper comment?" J1 says.

I reach in my pocket for my phone, but N3 grabs my arm.

"People don't give Jesus enough credit for being a badass," J1 says. "Sure, the whole washing of the feet thing, but think about it. The Last Supper is basically a bad gangster dinner." Then, in a poorly executed Brando-Godfather voice: "I dip this bread and give it to my betrayer, the bitch Judas. Here you go. No heaven for you. Oh, and another thing. Peter, you'll screw me over three times then a rooster will crow. Yes, I know that sounds weird as shit, but just wait you little fuck. Let's have some bread and wine. Yes?"

Laughing, N3 nods her head in approval, but I'm devastated. None of that on video.

"Deep breath, Marcos," J1 says. "Let's stay sane here."

I don't say anything. I look up through the trees and exhale.

What is this world?

This is nothing like Grozny.

"You pissed?" N3 says. "I'm too hard on you?"

I should say, "This is nothing. I've been through real initiation. Before the Domodedovo Airport bombing the Chechens made me strip naked and beat me with belts of wire. Only then could I film."

But that won't get me anywhere. I've stayed alive this long because I refuse to antagonize.

"No video," I say. "And that was gold," pointing at J1.

"For her shitty Godfather voice?" N3 says. "I don't think so."

"I'll do it again," J1 says, bouncing with some newly tapped energy.

"No," N3 says.

N3 tilts the rifle's barrel toward me, and when I look away, she raises the barrel under my nose.

"Smell," she says. "I know you like it."

I'd love to tell N3 to fuck off, but not this evening. I've never seen J1 jovial, and I don't know what to do with her new countenance. I know it'll be gone soon.

J1 stands close to me, dripping, energetic.

I pull out my iPhone and start a video. N3 doesn't say anything.

"What else do I know?" J1 says to herself. Then, to us: "Guess this." In what I think is supposed to be an Alicia Silverstone–Clueless voice, "Ah, yeah, like, Judas, ewww. You're a dick. You, too, Peter. Like, seriously. As if."

This voice isn't as good as the Brando, but it's miraculous all the same. She stares right at my iPhone. I watch J1 through my phone's screen, and I'm mostly present here at Echo Lake, absorbing the moment, but somehow I'm also in an empty auditorium on Chico State's campus two months earlier. J1 had only told me the basics about the militia in our encrypted e-mail correspondence, but it was enough to get me on a plane.

The auditorium was hot. I started video immediately, which took her off guard. She didn't know where to look: me, the iPhone, or past us into the empty rows. I never tell them where to look.

"I loved your work with the Zapatistas," J1 said.

I believed her.

"Just talk," I said. "I don't interrupt. I don't speak on video. When you're done, just stop talking. Before we get to Jefferson, start with yourself."

"So you're doing this?" she said.

I nod in the past and present.

"Bring it on," N3 says.

J1 shakes her head.

"As if," J1 emphasizes.

"Mean girls," N3 says.

"Really?" J1 says. "Marcos, you know. Guess."

I won't. The video rolls.

"Guess," J1 says, but I don't say anything. She waits several seconds, but she knows the deal. Yes, I could just edit my voice out later, but why? This isn't about me.

"Fucking guess," J1 says.

I mouth, "No."

J1's positivity skydives.

She's quick, volcanic.

"You think this is some dumb shit?" J1 says. "What's your problem?"

"Put the phone away, now," N3 says. "Enough."

"What is it, Marcos?" J1 says. "Too much to ask?"

She's radiant, angry, but always under control. This is her genius. It must have saved her in Chowchilla.

"A simple guess, motherfucker," J1 says. "Scared we'll get your voice on your precious doc?"

N3 swipes at my phone, but I keep rolling.

"You think we're doomed, don't you?" J1 says. "It's the only reason you're here."

Of course they're doomed, but maybe not tomorrow.

"J," N3 says.

"It's true," J1 says. "Why else would he be here?"

What is this, personal embarrassment? A ruined moment of repose? Awareness this might be her last night? Simple anger because I won't play?

And although I'd never tell her, of course her playacting isn't dumb. There's a long history of pre-attack nerves and methods of remedy: Napoleon demanded melody via a violinist, Stonewall Jackson—the night before Antietam—masturbated in the woods, Xerxes I purportedly drank lion blood from a golden cup. But I'm not here to grant assurances.

"Guess," J1 demands.

Her towel falls away.

N3 stands and grabs my arm.

"Fucking guess!" she says.

How unknowable we are, moment to moment. No one is exempt.

Years ago, in San Cristóbal de las Casas, Mexico, I photograph a band of Zapatistas as they overrun jails and release hundreds of prisoners. Chaos and desperation and rapture. I run out of the burning city as fast as I can to keep up with the jeeps. At the edge of town I see one of the prisoners playing marbles with children in a newly sown field, gunfire everywhere.

Outside Grozny, three hours before she straps on a suicide vest, Sasha removes my condom and we make love for the last time.

And now, why won't I answer?

J1 takes another step towards me and presses her stomach against my phone.

In the near distance I see Jones running out of Echo Lake towards me. How has the day turned into this?

I close my eyes. I am the iPhone's video feed, blacked out and listening.

N3 presses the AR-15 into my side.

J1's breath is on me. I feel her body shake as it tries to warm.

"Guess," J1 whispers into my ear. "As if."

Someone rips the phone from my hand.

"Guess," J1 says.

Guess. Guess. Guess. The word floats in the darkness of my mind, throws me back to 1999 when I'd play the game TENDONS on an iMac. After double-clicking the TENDONS icon the screen popped up a series of photos of people with their eyes closed. Underneath the photo, the game commanded: Guess.

I had two choices: Asleep or Dead.

Because they're photos it was nearly impossible to tell. No soft movement of the rising and dropping chest. No eye fluttering. But once in a while a poorly cropped photo appeared, and I'd notice blood on a shoulder or the disc of a stethoscope. Click: Dead.

Someone grabs the back of my neck and squeezes.

"Take his shoes off," J1 says.

"What the fuck?" Jones says.

"Crow," J1 says.

"Me?" Jones says. "Crow? The bird?"

"Not you," N3 says.

"As if," J1 says. Her mouth on my ear. Her warm breath. "As if. Guess."

Photo: an old Japanese woman, mouth wide open. Head on a blue pillow. A glass of water nearby. A book on a side table. Guess. Click: Asleep.

Photo: a young man, maybe sixteen, shaved head. Left ear resting on left shoulder. On his brown shirt collar, dried white spittle. A clear tube into his left arm. Guess. Click: Dead.

Video: Sasha buttons the top button of her Adidas coat and touches my face. She steps into the back of a black van, and it drives away. Guess. Click: Dead.

"Guess," J1 says.

Is the video running? Will it pick this up? Will anyone find it?

N3 laughs. No doubt she gets off on my fear.

"Clueless," I whisper.

"What?" J1 says. "I can't hear you. Is that your guess?"

I open my eyes and J1 stands in front of me, naked, knife in hand.

"Clueless." I say.

N3 shoves the barrel deeper into my side, and my arms flail out. Jones wraps his arm around my neck and squeezes.

"No," J1 says. "That's wrong."

She reaches out and pushes the tip of the knife into my chest.

I can't breathe. I will die here. California. Echo Lake. April.

She lowers the knife and smiles.

"That's enough, Jones," she says.

"What?" he says.

"It's okay," J1 says.

He releases his choke, and I double over, gasping.

"Through the mouth," J1 says. "You're no rookie, Marcos. Come on. Breathe. Here, sit."

N3 pushes me into the folding chair.

"Jones," J1 says, "go dress. We're good here."

A bottle of water lands in my lap. I drink.

"No one remembers the quiet," J1 says. "I want your film to do well, Marcos. You need me to be who I am. You need my backstory. You need what just happened here. I know where you've been. You use people, and I like that. But you're going to tell the story we want you to tell."

J1 stands and walks over to N3. I take the opportunity to regain myself, the silent self-talk that this is nothing new. I've been through worse. Perseverance is all about the clever lies we tell ourselves.

I need to recover fast, and I'm ready to believe.

When J1 returns she hands me my iPhone.

"Start video," she says.

I hit record, and J1 stands up straight.

"Ask me anything," she says. "I want to hear your voice."

I never asked Sasha her name. The leaders called her BB, so I did, too. I found her real name on the front page of *The Moscow Times* after the bombing. Alongside the article was a photo of a man dressed for his burial. The photo only shows his upper half. He is young and still. His eyes are closed. He wears a black suit, white shirt, black tie. He is recently shaved. If you look close you can see his cracked lips and a recent cut, along his jaw, that will never heal.

Sometimes Kids Bleed
for No Reason

You don't haunt me. Not at my daughter's soccer games or when I dodge a deer in my Chevy on the outskirts of Elko. You don't come to me in my dreams or surprise me when some neighborhood girl dresses up as Little Red Riding Hood for Halloween. But it's true, some mornings as I sip my chai and drop an Oxy and watch my front lawn in the morning light I imagine that I met you in the village east of Ramadi, where we'd go when we didn't want any shit, where we'd go and hand out candy to the swarming kids, then watch them play soccer all hopped up on peppermint and butterscotch rounds. I see you and your red hijab there among the chaotic darting and shouting, the worn soccer ball, the out-of-bounds lines etched in dirt. In my morning vision there's no dust storms, no Humvees, no snipers, just you and the games east of Ramadi. But that's not where we met.

A week before I first saw you, before I felt you, another goddamn ambush in the city. We'd been warned that they were forcing kids out into the middle of the street as bait.

I rode in the backseat when a gap-toothed boy smiled and waved, and Martin stopped the Humvee, the boy touching our idling bumper, and I saw the dirt on his face before he ditched into the alley, just before the RPGs and AKs and *Allahu Akbars* ripped the afternoon open. My friend Liggins took a bullet to his head and I held his skull together with my hands as we sped away. His green eyes were on me and his head leaked out a clear liquid that soaked my fingerless gloves and I watched him die as I held his head together, my hands on the sides of his head, my fingertips in his wet hair.

That shit makes you want to live, and for a week I woke thinking about my skull and legs and dick and hands and skin, thinking of how to keep the stuff inside me inside. The images and smells of home tried to destroy me—the gold mine, the outline of Mt. Elko, the rancher Jen and I bought just before my deployment, Jen's new tits in my hands, the smell of my daughter after her bath, watching 49ers football in my living room—but I had two months left in Iraq and I knew one day I'd have to drive down the avenue that took Liggins, so when the officers ordered all of us to keep our feet off the goddamn brakes, no exceptions, we cheered.

The day before I first saw you, before I felt you, I called Jen with my feet in the Euphrates and told her about Liggins and I begged her not to put little Katie on because I couldn't take it, but she told me our daughter needed to hear my voice, so I waited as the phone went quiet and I heard *Dora the Explorer* in the background, then Jen's voice, *It's daddy*, then Katie's breathing. She was two and I said, *Are you watching Dora?* but I only heard her breathing, and I imagined her just bathed and towel-wrapped, shaking her head at Jen in our newly painted living room, waving off my voice.

That night I thought about Liggins, how when we got back to post after the attack the docs told me to take my hands off his head but I couldn't move, and when I finally made it back to my room how I smelled my hands before I washed them, how everyone said *At least he didn't have a family* like that somehow made things easier, how I was one of the few that really knew him, how he loved Tom Petty, how before he signed up he was a baker in Orlando and he swore that Tiger Woods would come into the bakery every other week and buy a dozen snickerdoodle cookies. He loved waking in the dark, the grease and flour and butter on his hands. *It's perfect*, he told me, *No one comes into a bakery pissed off unless you misspell their kid's name on a birthday cake.*

The day I saw you, the day I felt you, I drove the lead vehicle through Ramadi, peppermint and butterscotch lodged in my right pocket, a Rockstar energy drink blaring through my veins. Electrical wires everywhere. Gunfire in the distance, white clouds and contrails, beat up Datsuns and old hags selling chai. And then, you. You stepped out into the street and showed your face to the sky. You were twelve, maybe thirteen years old, a red hijab, your mouth open in the street, your hands nursing a soccer ball, your hands spinning the black and white hexagons in the heat, in the July sun, in the dirty street, your mouth open, facing us, turning the soccer ball in your hands, watching us as we closed fast, speeding, your mouth open in Ramadi, gunpowder and dust in the air, you were twelve, maybe thirteen, a red hijab, standing in the street. Did you think we would stop? Is that what they told you?

You should see Katie on Saturday mornings. We pull her brown hair back into a ponytail so her hair doesn't get in her eyes. She's four now and her soccer team is called the Tigers, and she's horrible. She picks clovers during the action and never kicks the ball in the right direction so the coach barely plays her. A couple weeks ago, one of her teammates accidentally kicked the ball into her face and Katie fell over bawling. I wanted to leave her there until she stood on her own, but Jen ran out onto the field and picked her up. There's no learning in that, and I know the lie Jen whispered as she brought Katie to the sideline, *It's okay. It's all okay.*

Driving the Humvee was easy. Twenty feet out you raised the soccer ball above your head. I felt my wet hands on Liggins. I felt my skull and legs and dick and skin and I felt the lurch of the Humvee as I mashed the gas. Someone was yelling *Fuck*, *Fuck*, and you with your open mouth, your red hijab, a moment before I felt you.

I felt you in the twitch of the steering wheel. I felt you in the gentle push of my body into the seat. I felt you in the adrenaline rush that told me I was whole.

You don't haunt me. Not when I hear *Dora the Explorer*. Not when I drive by BJ Bull bakery on my way to work. Not when Katie takes another soccer ball to the face or when I bathe her and she reaches for me when it's time to get out. Not when I watch CNN and see that al-Qaeda has recaptured Fallujah and fucking McCain says we never should have left.

People told me you were retarded, that they only force the fucked-up ones to stand in the street, and I've tried to imagine you stupid and flailing, an idiot rambling to your soccer ball in the heat, but that's not you. Sometimes

I follow you to your street, to your home, and watch you wrap the hijab around your head and reach down for the soccer ball and open the front door on that July morning. I've pictured you at school, writing your name, the right-to-left Arabic, you write your name, but I can't read it. I don't know what to call you.

The other day Jen and I took Katie out to River View Park and walked the path by the Humboldt River. We watched Katie ride her bike with training wheels, joggers passing by, and Jen reached for my hand and said, *Please talk to me*, so I told her about the time Martin and I wowed a hundred Iraqi kids with only a Nerf football, but when I finished she said, *That's not what I meant*, and looked away. She looked away because she doesn't know the right questions to ask, she doesn't get why I call Martin every month, doesn't get that I'm content with my construction job, that I don't need the VA to help me with shit. She believes in forgetting, encourages me to wipe away the bad stuff, but I tell her she's wrong, the crazy only starts when you try to forget. She looked away by the Humboldt because she doesn't understand that the only real love you can have for someone is killing for them. Dying is easy.

I'll never wish my 412 days in Iraq away. There's beauty everywhere. I walked Saddam's marble palaces and stole a miniature sword and put my boot through a plaster wall in one of his bathrooms. During downtime I smoked as we pit scorpions against camel spiders and cheered as they circled in on one another. I cursed the sun and warm drinking water and the freezed up Skype connection. I watched porn and UFC fights and the nightly news that never mentioned shit about us. I dodged sandstorms, but I stood outside and felt the swirling sand and grit as the helicopter airlifted Liggins away. I listened to the calls to prayer from the minarets and cranked "Free Fallin'" when I wanted to feel strong.

My mother drives up from Vegas every now and then and watches Katie so Jen and I can have some time to ourselves. Almost always we drive to the Red Lion Casino in town and play the slots. Jen once bagged five-hundred bucks on a dollar machine. We ate platefuls of crab legs in the restaurant and lost the rest at roulette and we were happy. Each time before she leaves my mother pulls me aside and brings up therapy. I know Jen puts her up to it. It doesn't bother me. They'll never understand that you were all I needed. I wanted you there in the street. I wanted to be driving. My God it felt amazing smashing you into the fucking road and driving away.

Each night I watch Katie sit in the bath and finger the water's surface. In the corner are makeshift bathtub toys: a yellow plastic ring, a miniature Dora and dump truck, a rubber Nevada magnet I bought in the airport on the trip home. When she grabs the magnet she looks at me and shouts "Nevada!" because she knows I'll smile. One night after I dried her off I found a small blood streak on the towel so I inspected her head to toe, but I couldn't find anything wrong. I was frantic and Jen came in and told me to calm down, that sometimes kids bleed for no reason, but that's not true.

A week after I saw you, after I felt you, we went back to the village east of Ramadi, passed out candy, and watched the games. Martin ripped on the 49ers and squeezed my neck and asked how many times I'd been to Salt Lake, but nothing was working so he brought out his Nerf football and all at once the kids stopped everything and watched us throw the ball back and forth, the football flying through the desert air. A hundred kids, maybe more. Quiet. Wowed.

Katie likes to watch the 49ers games with me on Sunday afternoons, and when I head to the back porch at the end of each quarter for a Lucky Strike she follows me outside and watches me smoke. She knows not to come near me, so she sits in the wicker chair and counts how many times I exhale. When it's cold she breathes out like me, puffing her own little breath clouds. Jen has never asked me to quit smoking, only to keep Katie away. I know what I'm doing. The worst thing you can say about someone is they don't know what they're doing. I know what my lungs will look like near the end.

I won't think of you at Katie's high school graduation or her wedding or if Jen and I hit another jackpot at the casino or if we decide to have another kid. You're not the reason I'll kick the Oxy or give in and agree to walk in the Fourth of July parade this summer with the other vets down Main Street. Not everyone comes home fucked up.

In the mornings I look at my front yard—a healthy chunk of grass, a few growing pines, and a small chicken coop we put up last fall—and although we bought this place I wonder what we own. The front yard? The trees? The air above our house? Jen thinks the chicks will survive the winter, and I hope she's right. We've got one of Katie's drawings up on our refrigerator, green crayon mountains, and "Katie," in purple, spelled out perfectly. There's beauty everywhere.

It's true, sometimes I imagine I met you east of Ramadi. Sometimes you're among the kids playing soccer. Sometimes you're sucking on a peppermint candy, one of the hundred kids watching Martin wind up and throw the football to me. You're not sure what's happening with these soldiers and this odd ball. You don't know that Liggins is dead. You don't know I have two months until I can go home and breathe. You don't know that sometimes war is the answer.

God's Zipper

Caleb, a US Air Force A-10 pilot, calls me at 1 a.m. Tallahassee time. It's early October 2014. I know better than to ask where he's calling from. He begins, as always, with the point.

"I killed 23 Taliban," he says. "But it's hard to tell the exact number."

He pauses. We've done this enough times at this hour of night, and he knows I need to move. Sarah and our kids sleep.

I keep the lights off, slide out of bed, and tiptoe out into the garage. Unusually warm, the garage barely contains our two cars, kids' bikes, mounds of sports gear, gardening tools I rarely use, and unopened boxes from our last move. Somewhere in here, an old Air Force Academy jacket. Caleb would have his, too. He lets nothing go.

"I'm here," I say.

"It's better when I fly at night," he says. "Even with night vision it's still mostly dark. Easier to stay calm."

I think, but don't say: Where are you, my dear friend?

On the flight line?

In your bunk?

When's the last time you've had a good meal?

"I'm not tired," he says. "That's the thing. All the training and warnings and shit. Everyone says, 'You'll get tired. Be careful when you're tired.' I'm wide awake. And it's not the 'go pills' they give us. I'm just awake."

"You're sleeping?" I say.

"So much of the land out here looks like Nevada. It's amazing. If you didn't tell me otherwise I'd think I was in the Ruby Mountains."

Then silence.

"Caleb?" I say.

"Duke is going to suck this year," he says.

I don't question the abrupt transition. We often escape to the subject of college basketball, the spectacle that has pulled us in for years with its young giants and imaginary stakes.

He curses Mike Krzyzewski, the Blue Devil program, and "drastically overrated" freshman Jahlil Okafor.

Caleb grew up poor in Nevada, but he roots for the Kentucky Wildcats.

"Sure, John Calipari is a criminal, but he doesn't hide it," Caleb says.

"Krzyzewski's a West Point grad lest you forget."

"Just stop," Caleb says. "You think his assistants aren't doling out money? You think Okafor is there for the education? Stop."

"You sleeping?" I say.

"Calipari doesn't hide it," he says. "He isn't scared of the NCAA or punishment or giving back titles. And guess what? Not one Kentucky fan cares. Calipari knows his audience, man. I love it."

"I hear you," I say. "When's the last time you slept?"

"The sun's out."

"Okay," I say. "You got some 'No Go's on you?'"

"Blue Devils suck," he says.

In the late 1990s Caleb and I endure military survival training together in the Colorado Rocky Mountains: 9,000 feet above sea level, little food, little sleep, cold nights, rudimentary navigation skills, and obscenities. The training supposedly prepares us in case we're ever shot down behind enemy lines. The third member of our trio is from Houston and has never been camping, let alone read a map. We call him Houston. He keeps hugging himself.

After some instruction on the foundations of staying alive and keeping quiet, we're on our own. The goals are fairly simple: survive for a few days and don't get too lost.

"If you hit Canada you've gone too far," an instructor says, a joke we're too tired to acknowledge.

Before they leave us, the instructors provide our small group a single rabbit.

"It's up to you," one instructor says with a bit of last-minute advice, "but I wouldn't name it. Soon you'll be hungry enough."

The instructor shows us how to kill the rabbit with a broken-off tree branch. In her left hand she holds the rabbit by the hind legs, head down, and strokes the rabbit's back with the branch.

"This calms it. You see how the body stretches out? There, there, rabbit. Now, the strike must be fierce and to the back of the neck at the base of the skull. Listen, dumbshits, we're not barbarians. One hit on target and it's over quick."

She mimes the strike.

Houston steps back.

"There's a lot of ways to fuck this up," she said. "Don't be that person."

Air Force Vernacular:
"Go Pill" = Dexedrine
"No Go Pill" = Ambien

The Chasseurs Alpins—nicknamed "les Diables Bleus"—were renowned, alpine-trained French soldiers during World War I. Relied upon to break the bleak stasis of trench warfare in their native region of the French Alps, the Vosges Campaign in March 1915 failed to change the status quo, even though the Blue Devils won accolades for their courage.

The Blue Devils' distinctive blue uniform with flowing cape and jaunty beret captured public imagination. When the United States entered the war, units of the French Blue Devils toured the country helping raise money in the war effort.

Duke University adopted the mascot name in 1922.

Caleb is in ninth grade. He's eaten saltine crackers and peanut butter for his last three meals. His mother, long gone to Mississippi. His father, becoming more unhinged, drives Caleb to an abandoned silver mine outside Austin, Nevada. This is not unusual. They both carry hand axes and five gallon buckets. The wooden braces of the mine have splintered over the years, but it's a place they both know well. Their small headlamps project onto the rock walls.

They work hard for three hours then Caleb's father hands him a Snickers bar, a rare luxury. The chocolate, nougat, peanuts, and caramel intoxicate him.

As Caleb tells it, he is in mid-Snickers-bar-chew when his father shouts, "Shithellbitchhell!"

Not shit. Not hell. Not bitch. Not hell again. One word, Shithellbitchhell.

His father's tone is feverish. Caleb runs to his father who is bent over, already hysterical.

—z—

Afghanistan. A radio call from ground troops in trouble. Taliban fighters with the high ground. Amphetamined up and ready, Caleb banks hard and fast in his A-10 aircraft, unleashing rounds from the herculean 30mm cannon. Three firing passes in the foothills of the Hindu Kush then cheers from the radio. American and Afghan soldiers will live tonight.

Later, Caleb's commander tells him the subsequent ground patrol and daytime satellite photos can't accurately capture the carnage. "As close as we can tell, the number is 23," his commander says, "Beautiful and horrible, but more beautiful."

—z—

Gold in a silver mine, that's what Caleb's father finds. The ore is as big as his fist. He names it Shithellbitchhell.

—z—

We don't listen to our survival instructor. I name the rabbit Laettner. Caleb names the rabbit Wildcat.

It takes 12 hours without food before Houston asks if it's time to get a tree branch.

"Not yet," Caleb says, knowingly. "Hunger doesn't kick in for 48 hours. Anyways, there's plenty of wild onions."

"Maybe we can fatten him up," Houston says. "What do rabbits eat?"

"For being so stupid," Caleb says, "you're killing Wildcat when it's time."

"Laettner," I say, secretly relieved no one has fingered me as the killer.

⁓

Caleb's father has the ore appraised.

$6,500.

For Caleb, it's too large a sum to fathom. He can't fight off visions of subjective grandeur: a new mobile home maybe, enough propane to keep them warm through the winter, steel toe boots he'll keep forever, pants that fit, laundry detergent whenever they want, unexpired food.

But then something staggering occurs—the ore sits on his father's bedside table for a week, then two, a month. Caleb's father stops shaving, sips Old Crow whiskey, snacks microwave popcorn, watches and re-watches VHS recordings of *The Price is Right* and *Wheel of Fortune*. Caleb questions his father once and is told to stay quiet about the damn gold. The second time Caleb presses—What are you doing? Why don't you cash it in? What the hell is wrong with you?—and he begins to sob.

"Next time you ask about it," his father says, "You got no place to live."

⁓

"You saved dozens, my friend," I say into the phone.

It's 1:17 a.m. Caleb has taken a brief pause on his Duke hating.

I walk around inside my garage as I listen to him describe the engagement.

American and Afghan ground troops pinned down.

Only 25 meters from the Taliban fighters.

Four of ours already injured.

Can't hold out much longer.

Circling in the plane.

Only 25 meters.

No room for error.

Radio transmission: Where are you? and the pop pop pop in the background.

This is real.

It's easy to know it's real.

Anyone says it's like a video game is full of shit.

Trained, yes, but thrilled, calm, nervous, thrilled, calm, nervous.

The Gatling gun shakes the plane.

The sound, God's zipper.

Radio transmission: On target! Again! Again!

That radio voice.

You can't imagine.

Exultation.

That voice in my ear.

I find a new scratch on our Honda Pilot. My fingernail catches as I inspect the gouge.

"It's fucked up how something you're proud of can mess with you," Caleb says. "It's not like I regret it at all. Hell, I'm lucky. This was a clear bad guy situation. I wouldn't do anything different."

"Twenty-three," I say.

"Yeah," Caleb says. "Michael Jordan's number."

"That's one way to think about it."

"The easiest way," he says. "I'd do it again. I'm glad it

was me. And you ask me if I can sleep. You wouldn't be able to sleep."

—z—

Duke will win the National Championship in the 2014–2015 season. Okafor immediately enters the NBA draft. He is selected third.

—z—

Randy Gardner is the holder of the record for the longest a human has gone without sleep. In 1964, Gardner, a high school student in San Diego, California, stayed awake for 264.4 hours (11 days 25 minutes).

—z—

Caleb has Shithellbitchhell. He stole it a few weeks before his father died, not that his father would have noticed at that point. He was too far gone into some horrific combination of dementia and liver-pancreas cancer. Caleb keeps the ore in a small safe beneath his bed.

Once, when I'm visiting him in Arizona, he shows Shithellbitchhell to me. His hands can't stop shaking, but he won't let me hold the gold.

"Don't ask me how much it's worth," he says. "I don't know."

The ore is dark gray with fantastic, thick veins of gold spidering everywhere.

"In a silver mine," I say, and shake my head.

"I was eating a Snickers," Caleb says.

We stand in his bedroom for a few minutes looking at the ore. He turns it in his unsteady hands.

—z—

After the Air Force Academy I begin a job in logistics. Training in Texas. An assignment in England then New Mexico. I'm in Albuquerque when I open an e-mail from Caleb. He's just graduated from the latest phase of pilot training and has discovered which aircraft he will fly.

The subject line: Warthog!

After two and a half days of eating wild onions in the Rockies Caleb says it's time to kill Wildcat. We already have the broken tree branch. Houston has been holding the branch for half a day.

It's near dusk, and we've found a granite overhang to spend the night. We're safe and concealed and tired. We put down our gear and I start a small fire. I don't want to be close to this.

Caleb hands the rabbit to Houston. He's surprisingly eager. It's the hunger and fatigue.

"Thanks, Wildcat," Caleb says. "You will fill us with energy."

Then, to Houston, "You can do this. Swing hard."

"I can do this," Houston says.

With his left hand Houston holds the rabbit by the hind legs and the rabbit jolts twice. Houston takes the branch and strokes the rabbit's back. Once, twice, and again. The rabbit lengthens and calms.

"Hard," Caleb says.

Houston lifts the tree branch high in the air. He swings and turns his head and groans, and he lifts the rabbit. The branch rushes below the rabbit's head. A miss.

"Shit!" Houston says.

"You can do this," Caleb says. "Again."

Houston exhales and grimaces. He walks in a small circle still holding the rabbit by the hind legs.

"Do it," Caleb says. "You got this."

"I got it," Houston says.

"Again," Caleb says.

Houston strokes the rabbit. Once, twice, along its spine. Again, he swings with his right hand and groans and yanks the rabbit up and misses low.

Caleb steps forward and grabs the rabbit. Houston trudges to the fire.

"Don't talk to me," he says.

"Jesse, you got to hold it," Caleb says. "Get over here."

"I'm not holding it," I say. "Come on. Just do it."

"Get over here," Caleb says. "Please."

It's the "please" that makes me stand. I walk over to Caleb, and although it's getting dark, I see his eyes well up.

"That guy's never been hungry," he says. "Never."

"Caleb," I say.

"You've got to hold it," he says. "I wouldn't ask…"

Caleb hands me the rabbit.

The rabbit is heavy in my hands.

We shouldn't have named it.

"Houston's never been hungry," Caleb says. "When's he been hungry?"

I hold the rabbit away from my body.

"Never," Caleb says. "Never. Never."

Caleb strokes the rabbit with the branch.

"We're not hungry," he says.

I wait for him to stop, to raise the branch and swing.

"Not hungry," he says.

Again and again, he soothes the rabbit.

Begin with Serenity

I'm the three-year-old boy Ted Bundy saved from drowning in Green Lake, Washington during the summer of 1970.

And no, my rescue story didn't make it into the *New York Times* while Bundy's murder trial captivated millions down in Florida, and apparently he didn't have it in him to bring me up as he ranted and raved during his bizarre, I'll-serve-as-my-own-lawyer game in front of Judge Cowart. This was before they strapped Bundy into the electric chair and cranked the dial to 100.

I know you can't fathom that your 48-year-old neighbor in Ely, Nevada, is the breathing manifestation of benevolence from a mass murderer. And what do you expect me to say after all these years, that he was a hell of a guy? He was incapable of love or generosity? Maybe you think he should have let me sink to the bottom of Green Lake.

Yes, that's what you want—you and all of the parents of the dead. I see your fantasy: Bundy on the shore eating a pastrami sandwich, grinning between bites as he watches young Scott Kerwitz drown. You love the perverse joy he bathes in, how lucky he is to be here, in this moment, and all he has to do is chew and watch this small boy wade out into the water.

You want me to confess the complicated elation of my existence—that's what you want. You see me only in opposition to the thirty or so women Bundy killed. You stalk me at Gale Oil and Tire, at the Railway Museum, at the White Pine Golf Course, in the Copper Park apartments. You stand behind me as I stare into my bathroom mirror on the worst days of my life, steak knife in hand, and whisper, "Do it."

—

I wander off from my parents' picnic blanket, my father dozing, my mother mesmerized by page 172 of *The Andromeda Strain*. The sparkled light from the shallows draws me in. It's July, and Seattle is cloudless, but the lake is still cold, so I ease in, then stop and stand waist-deep. The ambient sounds of splashing, gulls, and laughter lull me to imbalance.

The first breath is liquid, muddy, explosive.

I'm my pleading lungs.

I'm in Bundy's arms.

I'm alive.

Consolable.

—

What do you need to know? Some things I can explain: I'm six-foot-two, two-hundred pounds, a guilty Catholic, a straight-up tax man, an old-school baseball fan. I've been married and divorced twice, and both Kathy and Zadie will tell you I'm great for the first four years then, like most people, I'm prone to complacency.

"You settle, Scott," Kathy said.

"Who doesn't?"

"But you settle *with vigor.*"

It's no sin. At least we didn't make things worse with kids.

I earned a Master's in Education at Saint Martin's University, but I couldn't live with your ugly elementary school children and their snot-stained hands and incessant whining, so I jetted off to Ely, the middle of nowhere. I now work enough hours at H&R Block to get the 1040s right and take home adequate money for golf, my cherished fishing trips, and the occasional bottle of Dalwhinnie scotch.

The arts: I prefer the Rolling Stones over U2, *Blade Runner* over *Platoon.*

The body: I once had a two-inch benign tumor removed from my collarbone. My left foot goes numb after four drinks.

Temperament: I refuse to eat any animal I respect.

Belief: God exists, but pain is a better motivator.

Growing up, during the summer months, I'd go with my professor father to the University of Washington and sit impatiently in the back of the classroom as he lectured on marine life, hatcheries, how one could determine the health of salmon by the shades of pink on their insides. Yes, boring as hell.

Other days, I walked with my mother to Omni Yoga where she'd greet her poorly attended classes with "Let's begin with serenity," then softly sing "Down Dog," "Crescent Moon," "Lotus," "Warrior." It's not her awkward poses that have stayed with me all these years, but the tenor of her voice—inviting, warm—all the while knowing about the savage world outside the yoga studio's walls.

How does a person summon peace like that, and in front of strangers?

You can tell a lot about a person they way they sit down to do their taxes with you. You have the clueless, who think they're going to strike it rich with their returns even though they fouled up their withholdings; the angry, who already know capital gains/inheritance tax/no receipts are going to destroy them; the organized, who should be doing their own paperwork.

They're all universally impatient. You can feel it in their thinly disguised contempt for my work, as if I'm the IRS myself. For the worst I reserve my mother's yoga greeting with a slow sarcastic twist: "Let's begin with se-ren-i-ty." You can see the bewilderment on their faces. *Serenity*. They haven't heard the word in a decade, and surely, not in a billion years did they expect to encounter it here, a day before Tax Day, in a cubicled H&R Block on East Aultman Street.

Again, I wander off from my parents' picnic blanket, my father dozing, my mother mesmerized by page 172 of *The Andromeda Strain*. The sparkled light from the shallows draws me in. I remember none of this, of course, but the scene haunts me occasionally in dream, or when I find a photo of my fourth birthday party at Chuck E. Cheese, or, vividly, in my most susceptible moments as I look at my bathroom mirror and try to push away thoughts of suicide by recalling my mother's soothing voice.

But there I am again, ankle deep in Green Lake.

Curious.

Near death.

Bundy could have stayed put. He could have held me under. I wonder if it was hard—his choice in the lake I mean—two pounds of pressure up or down.

You want me angry, I know it, but I don't owe those murdered women anything. My joy isn't their joy. They are not with me when I hold the door open for an old lady at True Value Hardware or bask in the ecstasy of another gulp of Dalwhinnie.

Zadie was the better wife. She was fearless, which scared the hell out of me. She'd been in the Coast Guard and could hold her breath for two and a half minutes, a skill she used to torture local lifeguards. On our honeymoon in San Diego she performed the Heimlich maneuver on a choking surfer at an In-N-Out Burger, but the chunk of burger wouldn't dislodge. The guy just went limp in her arms after a minute. The worst part was I could hear Zadie cracking the guy's ribs because her fist was a few inches too high. It took her three days to shake the adrenaline and fear.

She was a movie buff, especially war movies, most of which do nothing for me. *Saving Private Ryan* is a joke after the landing at Normandy. There are moments in *Platoon* where the actors don't seem afraid at all. I hate that. All war movies should employ unknown actors and demand a single mood in every scene: terror. My uncle served in Vietnam and he disagrees. He says he experienced terror, sure, but also every other conceivable emotion while on foot patrol. My uncle says that there's no such thing as war—that every day is the same, whether in Denver or Da Nang—we're all just trying to survive the day. That sounds wise and wrong.

I try to avoid knowing about them—Bundy's victims I mean—but what am I supposed to do, forget everything?

Am I not supposed to google each and every one of them and compare the potential of their lives to the reality of mine?

One of them was named Brenda, the same name as my boss at H&R Block. It shouldn't bother me, I know. Completely different people, you say. That may be true, but they're both equally inescapable. I call my boss "B" and it doesn't help one damn bit.

The day the doctors found the collarbone tumor, before we knew if it was malignant or benign, I hopped on a copper mine tour, one of those $100 for two hours traps for the tourists that want to see how deep we can gouge the earth. I wanted to feel small, and nothing does the trick like a pit. Some idiot kid was running the show and he didn't know the first thing about mining. Still, everyone snapped pictures of the gigantic trucks hauling out the good stuff.

It's a hell of a thing to wait on a biopsy result. You're waiting for a single word. It's even worse to realize the doctors don't know anything about cancer because it isn't even a thing, or at least not one type of thing. I've read *The Emperor of All Maladies*. Here's what I learned: (1) anything unexplainable in your body is cancer and (2) if you live long enough, you'll get cancer. If you're lucky something else will kill you first.

You might never guess Rock & Roll would be the thing to end you. I once saw a documentary on the Rolling Stones. They were playing this free concert near San Francisco and mayhem quickly ensued while the Stones rocked through their set. For some reason the Hell's Angels were in charge of security, and fights broke out everywhere, which was alarming, but solvable, and Mick Jagger stopped the band

and implored the crowd to calm down, but no one did, and people started dying. One person was stabbed, others trampled, and you can see the terror on Jagger's face as he gets the word and runs from the stage.

We all know every hero story requires a villain. It was my parents' fault, of course. You don't doze off or zone out in a Michael Crichton novel while your three-year-old slowly heads for the lake. What did they expect, someone else to notice?

You have to remember, for a time, the name Bundy was venerated in my house, and then the news came out about Bundy-the-murderer. The *Seattle Times* picked up the story. My parents' first reaction was disbelief: not *that* Ted Bundy, *our* Ted Bundy. My parents seemed horrified, which I understood, but in the days and weeks that passed—oddly, confoundedly—they projected something akin to relief. At least that's how I interpreted their obsessive interest in Bundy's subsequent trial. Maybe it was that we'd never have to talk about Green Lake again, or if we did, everyone would be guilty.

The two inch tumor grew on the inner facing part of my collarbone. I envisioned the mass of cells growing toward my heart with purposeful direction. Heart cancer—something you never hear. Lung cancer, breast cancer, colon cancer, prostate cancer. All common, all discussed, worried about, feared, but not heart cancer. I knew this lump would reach my heart, wrap itself around the beating muscle, and squeeze. Trust me, you would too. I touched my collarbone incessantly, even though I knew couldn't feel the tumor. It drove Kathy nuts, but what was I supposed to do? I eventually rubbed my skin raw.

I was called with the biopsy result, not by the doctor, but

by her assistant. It was a Tuesday in February. Kathy and I were about to walk into the Cellblock Steakhouse. She'd just made a big sale at the jewelry store and was telling me about the incredible size of the diamond in between puffs on her latest Marlboro. When the phone rang I sat down on a concrete bench. Kathy put out her cigarette, but she never reached for me.

"I have good news, Mr. Kerwitz," the assistant said.

Google benign. You might be surprised. The medical definition "not harmful in effect" comes after the word's primary meaning, "gentle; kindly." Example provided, "Her face was calm and benign." The nuance between the two meanings is stunning, if confusing. One use is medically defined only as a lack of something harmful, the sentence and power of malignant. The other, explicitly positive. But how can a face be gentle, kindly?

What do you need to know? My worst days arrive less frequently now. Who knows why I've had visions of all the parents of the murdered women cheering me on as I slice my wrists with a steak knife? Why am I always in my bathroom? Who is this ghost that looks at me in the mirror? And why, of all things, is it my mother's voice that brings me back each time? Will she always come when I need her?

Have I not been clear enough? If Kathy or Zadie and I had a child and that child was kidnapped, raped, and killed, I wouldn't want the criminal to face the death penalty. Hell, the electric chair or some toxic injection seems way too easy. I'd want that person to endure constant and prolonged torture, would wish for everlasting anguish, and during the brief moments between sessions, soul-destroying fear of forthcoming pain.

Ted Bundy's last words were "I'd like you to give my love to my family and friends." It's something you might say when the time comes.

Earlier, when I said that one of Bundy's victims was named Brenda, that's not true. Two were named Brenda. One was fifteen. One was twenty. Does it matter?

Again, I wander off from my parents' picnic blanket, my father dozing, my mother mesmerized by page 172 of *The Andromeda Strain*. The sparkled light from the shallows draws me in. I remember it all. It's a hot day in July, but the light isn't light, it's a million diamonds on the surface of the water. I can touch them if I rise, so I do. They're beautiful shifting diamonds right in front of me. I don't count my steps because they're right in front of me. I don't feel the cold water on my feet because I can touch them, these wet diamonds, they're everywhere.

Even at eight years old I have my own mat in the back of my mother's yoga class. There are only two or three people in the class with us, and they're already quiet. See my mother in an oversized Seattle SuperSonics T-shirt and black tights getting ready to start class. Her brown hair is in a ponytail and she's transitioned from a welcome-to-class smile to a focused, find-your-peace drowsiness. She looks at me and nods. This means everything is okay. This means we're about to start. She presses her palms together and breathes in. She will greet us soon. She will help us begin. I'm ready. I close my eyes and wait for her voice.

All Saints' Eve

It was Halloween, 1979, the day after Alicia's surgery for her ectopic pregnancy, so we kept the lights off in the house with the hope that everyone would leave us the hell alone. Silence was all we wanted. Birmingham was sweltering outside and we were both on our bedroom floor because Alicia said it was cooler on the carpet and it felt good on her back. She had showered for the third time that day and hadn't bothered to dry off or put on her robe, which I had never seen her do. Her head was in my lap and I ran my fingers through her wet hair, coaxing her to sleep.

I wished she'd have taken the damn drugs prescribed to her by the base doctor, but she refused. My legs ached and I could hear the distant sounds of children running and laughing up and down our street. My jaw clenched so tight I thought I would break my teeth. Alicia must have heard what I heard, but she didn't move, didn't say a word. I told myself I would slit their throats, each and every Superman, Bear Bryant, and Snow White, but Alicia's body relaxed and her breathing settled into a peaceful rhythm of sleep.

It was dark and the only sign that she was alive was her inhale-exhale sound. I hadn't slept much in the preceding days, but I wasn't tired even though I begged my mind to shut down. And there it came again, the screams and yelps of kids whining and begging. Alicia's head twitched and settled. I stopped stroking her.

In that same small room two months earlier she had told me she was pregnant. After a year of convincing me we should have kids, and another year trying, she had walked into the bedroom as I undressed. I was sitting on the edge of the bed taking off my black socks when she asked for my hands. I gave them to her, and she held them to her stomach.

"If it's a girl, Josie," she said. "A boy, Jaime." She always had something for the J names.

Alicia began to snore and I thought of how with every second that passed her body was healing, that something inside her was working hard to close the deep wound the doctor had cut through skin and fat and muscle and tube. I closed my eyes and sometime later I drifted off into a jumble of vivid memories and demented visions: my father lecturing me about how Alicia and I should have as many kids as possible because the "slackers" and "moochers" were overrunning the decent families in our state; the way I wanted my neighbor Martha when she brushed my arm after I helped her with a flat tire on her Cutlass; a homemade Snoopy costume of my childhood; a demented, big-nosed obstetrician turning to me during delivery and ordering me to bite the connected umbilical cord.

As I came to, I heard footsteps and chatter on our porch. I had sweated through my T-shirt and I looked for a clock but I couldn't see one. Alicia had moved her head from my lap and lay curled up on the floor next to me. I stood and the pain shot through my legs and back. I staggered out of the bedroom and stood in the hallway by the front door.

I heard the kids on our dark porch. It sounded like there were fifty, a hundred of them, whispering and gathering, sugared up and selfish. Why did they come up our driveway? Couldn't they see that no one was home? Not a single light on and no movement inside they could see, and yet here they were.

I stepped closer to the door and put my ear up to it.

Someone said, "Ring it."

Anger rushed at me, but why didn't I move? Why didn't I open the door and tell them to clear the hell out? Couldn't they see we didn't want them there?

Their feet shuffled on our porch, and again, that damn voice, "Ring it."

I knew Alicia was asleep on the floor and the doorbell would wake her. All I had to do was open the door and tell them to leave, but I stood in the hallway waiting for the sound, and when the ring came it arrived like a thunderclap. Once, then again, and still I stood there.

Over the years I've wondered about that night, about that minute I let the doorbell ring over and over, if I've made too much of my inaction, or if that was the moment when I should have known that I didn't love Alicia, at least in the ways that mattered, or that I didn't want kids, or if there was some other realization that should have hit me as I leaned against my front door doing nothing. I've never been able to make sense of it. There are many other, more pressing reasons why Alicia and I eventually divorced, including Martha, but that damn doorbell, only moments after I had been caring for Alicia, the emptiness of our hallway that one Halloween. I stood in the hallway and let it ring.

Finally, I heard the crowd walk away and I listened for Alicia. Around the corner, in our bedroom, a light turned on and I walked slowly toward it.

Alicia was lying across our bed on top of the covers. She was still. Her head was away from me and her knees were spread apart. The lamplight illuminated her lower half and I stared at the place where the doctors had shaved her pubic hair for the surgery, at the pale skin there and white bandage.

Alicia had always been hesitant with her nudity, even after three years of marriage. She never liked me to see her naked, early on telling me she was traditional. In practice this meant that she would ask me to turn away as she reached for a towel exiting the shower or bath. We made love exclusively in the dark, save for once on our honeymoon down at Destin. Even then, she turned around and looked out at the ocean. It was something I didn't fight, even though I always preferred to see her and not just feel her. So when I saw her in the lamplight I confess to being stunned at her nakedness. Even in that moment, already negotiating the guilt for the doorbell, and alongside thoughts of caring for her, healing her, I stared at her shaved body and thought of how I'd been inside her hundreds of times, but had never seen myself penetrate her, just feeling her in the darkness, and how difficult it had become to re-create Alicia's face and body underneath me during sex, how easy it was to imagine being with someone else—Iman, an old girlfriend at Tulane, and recently, Martha.

I did love Alicia, regardless of where my thoughts took me, regardless if I drove off the trick-or-treaters or not. She was strong, and I knew that her pain was not my pain, which saved me. Love requires attention, which I gave willingly, but not the fulfillment of every damn promise you make at twenty-six. How could it? Even now I don't regret the ridiculous offers I couldn't have understood nearly forty years ago: "If I could take away your pain and make it mine I would," "I know it will be okay," "I'll always be here."

I paused in the doorway and stared. This body in front of me was my wife. It was Halloween. It was hot. These were the things that I understood.

I walked to the lamp and reached out to turn it off, but before I did I glanced over at Alicia's face. Her eyes were open and she stared at the ceiling. Her mind was somewhere else, but where?

I thought of asking her if she wanted the drugs or a glass of water, but I said, "The damn doorbell. I'm sorry about that."

She didn't look at me, but she brushed her foot against my leg.

"Raul," she said. "We have to wait four months from today."

"Okay," I said. "Whatever you want."

I would have promised anything.

"End of February," she said, "we'll try again."

I've never cared for baseball, but in 1985 Bret Saberhagen was the hot topic as Mark and I started up our checklist in the ICBM silo thirty miles outside of Cheyenne. The Kansas City Royals had won the World Series a few days before and Saberhagen was the toast of the sporting world after winning the series MVP and becoming a father before his game seven shutout. It was something out of a movie script.

I was pulling a 72-hour alert shift with Mark, who was a big St. Louis Cardinals fan and, like me, a divorced Air Force Captain. He blamed the Cardinals' loss on an umpire's blown call, but he also gave Saberhagen his due, which I pretended to care about. There was nowhere to go.

We had the checklist down pat, both of us having had two years in the job—we each ensured that our main and backup power sources were good to go by pressing and releasing the white and green buttons at our consoles; we tested the intercom and phone lines by checking in with command dispatch; the pressure gauges were eye-level and spot on. Each of us unpacked our bags that contained more checklists, launch keys, secret codes, a change of clothes, food, toiletries, caffeine pills, books (*The Stand* for Mark, *Leadership for Now!* for me). That time, Mark was in charge of the porn and alcohol, and because I knew him well, it was no surprise when he proudly showed me a *Penthouse* and a bottle of Jack Daniels after everything else had been unloaded. The alcohol was for end-of-the-world scenarios.

What really happened when you pulled a 72-hour shift is you got bored as hell. Sitting underground, we'd run our initial checklist, make sure everything powered up just fine, then you'd sit there, call in every three hours, and try to stay awake until it was your turn to catch a few hours of sleep. Maybe you studied for a master's. Maybe you perfected yo-yo tricks. You might think we were stressed about Gorbachev or our possible role in killing innocent Russian babies or if we spent hours debating the merits of Stalin's *A single death is a tragedy; a million deaths is a statistic* or if we would really turn the key when the call came in, and sure, we thought about those things early on, intensely, in fact—I didn't want to kill anyone—but like anything, we got bored with the same stuff over and over, proving routine can destroy anything, it doesn't matter if it's pecan pie, a pair of shoes, or the consequences of controlling a nuke. Still, we took the important parts of the job seriously. We knew about the accidental launch over in Nebraska the previous year, as well as the Russian nuclear sub disaster that August that killed fifty of their sailors.

Unlike me, Mark had gained sole custody of his boy after his divorce, and a few hours into our shift I could tell that he was pissed at being stuck in the silo during Halloween. He had an aunt that had moved to Cheyenne to help him out with his boy, and Mark told me that was who was walking Steven around the neighborhood that night, and that Steven had dressed up as Ozzie Smith, the Cardinals' famous shortstop.

We'd been quiet for a few minutes after settling in, the World Series conversation long over, when Mark said, "Saberhagen's new kid will ruin him."

"I don't know," I said. "What does it have to do with pitching?"

"Sleep," he said.

Of course, my kid didn't ruin me, although I worried a lot about Jaime those days I spent in Wyoming. Alicia had stayed back in Birmingham with him, and I hated her for it. I hated her not because she divorced me, which she had the right to do after Martha confessed our affair to her one

morning, but because Alicia accurately predicted the guilt
I felt being an absentee father. Sure, I called Jaime on his
birthday and holidays and sent expensive presents I knew
Alicia couldn't match, but that was about it. That sinking
feeling Alicia predicted didn't hit me every day or every
time I passed a playground, not even when I spoke to Jaime
on the phone. Mainly it was down in that bunker when I
had nowhere else to go and too much time to kill. Invari-
ably, I'd be a day or two into the shift and the buttons and
blinking lights would start to drive me mad and I'd have
one of my reoccurring moments when I questioned who I
was and what was important to me. I knew how I was supposed to answer: "My boy, of course! I'll leave now, catch a
plane, repent, and spend the rest of my life being the father
I should be!" But that isn't how things worked. I knew I
could fight past the guilt of those attacking thoughts, and
I'd push through the shift and climb out of the bunker into
sunlight that always taunted loneliness, and I'd drive south
cranking Prince or Huey Lewis and the News, past miles
of empty fields and down into F. E. Warren Air Force Base
on the outskirts of Cheyenne. I don't know if it was the
music or landscape or tapping back into the world above
ground, but by the time I got to my front door I'd nearly
convinced myself that my boy didn't need me or that I'd
only ruin him if I went to visit. I had no reason to believe
this, and I can't explain why I felt that pressure to deny my
boy, no matter how rough it had gotten with Alicia. It was
all bullshit—that drive home, my woe-is-me solitude—but
retrospective judgment is easy. It's hard for me to recognize the person that made those choices. And why did it
take a tragedy to get me to change?

Around 8 p.m. Mark was in the bathroom with the *Penthouse* and I picked up the phone and checked in with dispatch. Like always, no news.

I cracked open *Leadership for Now!* and read a few pages, but each one seemed to scream the same crap: Confidence! Communication! Concentration! I'd been in the military long enough to know that most leaders succeeded because they took credit for other people's work. It was no secret.

Ten minutes later Mark came out of the bathroom.

"Got a thing for redheads, man," he said. "I don't know what it is."

"Yeah?"

"Something about the hair. I don't even care about their face."

"Wonderful to know you're not picky," I said.

"Something about it, man."

"It's rare, that's why."

"How old do you think that Wendy girl from Wendy's is?" he said.

"What the hell you talking about?"

"The restaurant," he said. "The burger place. The girl with the red hair on the signs. She's got to be twenty-five, thirty by now."

"The one with the pigtails?"

"Yeah, that's a real person you know. The founder's daughter I think. Can you imagine fucking her? You'd be thinking the whole time I'm fucking *the* Wendy."

"Yeah," I said.

"It'd be crazy. Pull that red hair back. My god."

"Probably rich as hell."

"Doesn't matter," he said.

"Maybe, but you'd drive by that sign and feel horrible, no matter how it went down. Have to always look at that little girl on the sign."

"What are you talking about?" he said. "That's a drawing. That isn't her. I'm talking about the real thing here. That Wendy, she's alive somewhere."

We were immature and heartless, but surely the word *war* is more obscene than *fuck*. We were stuck in a bunker, our only connection to the outside world a secure telephone line and intercom. No one was listening to us, and our filthy conversation would have disappeared from my memory were it not for the ringing phone that interrupted us.

Mark picked it up and I saw the horror overtake him.

"No," he said. "No. No."

What was he hearing? What was he denying?

He threw his head back and stood up, the phone to his ear.

"What?" he said. "What are you telling me?"

He stepped forward and punched the control panel.

"What are you telling me?"

For a few staggering moments I thought the call had finally come to launch our nuke, and in those seconds the fear ricocheted inside me.

In the dizziness and mayhem of those seconds I grabbed my launch key and opened the code sheet. I was scared, but I would do what I'd been trained to do.

Then I heard Mark scream, "Steven!"

The thing about an accident is that you never see it coming. If you did, you'd change something to stop it. That may seem obvious, but I've thought about that fact a lot. I heard the desperation in Mark's scream.

The questions rush at me still.

How were we to know that at the same time we were talking about red-haired Wendy Mark's son was stepping out into the street in front of that Chevy? It was impossible, and yet there's no absolution in what we couldn't know. And why did it take Steven's small coffin to get me to catch a plane to see my own son? I've told myself it was love, but it was always fear, even as the plane descended, even as Jaime hugged me after years away.

—✕—

In 1999 Alicia married again, and although the news of her engagement hadn't hit me too hard, save for a healthy dose of curiosity about the new man, something broke inside me the day of her wedding. The church ceremony was hundreds of miles away from me in Knoxville, but I was pissed off and irrational, and why not? I drove out to Las Vegas and got a room with two double beds on the thirtieth floor of The Mirage. The escort that showed up two hours after my call wore a kitten mask and a tight black leather dress and kept coughing in between introductory sips of Wild Turkey. The thrill that held me while waiting for her to arrive settled into regret with every one of her hacks. She told me her name was July, which made it worse. I smiled and tried to act at ease, but she must have been able to see the lie.

"We can do whatever you want," July said. "You want to talk for a while? I got 'til one."

July was taller than me and had curly brown hair. Even though I knew her movements were practiced it surprised me how comfortable she was sitting on the edge of the bed in the room near me. I sat on the other bed, our knees a foot apart. I felt the whiskey, but I knew where I was, even if I didn't know what I'd do.

"You talk," I said.

"Okay," she said. "Let me think."

"Are you from here?"

"What kind of story do you want?" she said.

"A happy story. Tell me about the best day of your life."

"You mean besides tonight?"

"Please don't do that," I said.

She smiled a practiced smile, full of straight teeth. Her coughing had stopped and she fingered the tab on her zipper that ran from her neck to her navel.

"A happy story?" she said and pulled the zipper down a few inches. "Okay, I met Mike Tyson at a party not too long ago. He was there and…where was it? Tampa? And I think Naomi Campbell was there too. Anyway, he was a really nice guy, and nothing happened, but that was a great night. They had this huge ice sculpture of a elephant right when you walked in, and it was so funny, everyone kept coming up to me saying, 'Pet the elephant. Pet the elephant.' But the elephant was melting. It was so funny."

She paused and looked over at me. She was telling the truth.

"I don't know. That's a happy story. It's random I guess, but it makes me laugh. 'Pet the elephant.' It was just ice. We weren't even drunk. I had some friends with me, and it was just cool, you know? No drama."

What did I expect, for her to confess she was a genius? That her best day involved loving parents and a trip to Disneyland?

We were quiet for a while. I couldn't escape the thought of Alicia on her second wedding night. Would we be having sex at the same time? At any time would she think of me?

I knew the questions were insane. Why did I care after so many years? I didn't want to get remarried. I didn't want Alicia back. But I wanted it to be true, that she would think of me, and longingly, even for a moment.

"What about you?" July said.

"I'm not a good storyteller."

"That's not fair. I tell you about Mike Tyson and you hold out on me?"

She twisted her face into an exaggerated pout.

I took another gulp of the Wild Turkey.

"Fine," I said, but I wasn't willing to confess anything. I searched for a good lie, and when none came to me, I said, "You mean besides tonight?"

I laughed at my own words.

"You never know," she said.

"Tell me about Tyson. Could I take him?"

"Oh, sure. Easily."

"He might bite my ear off," I said.

She had no clue about the Holyfield fight, and I could see the surprise come over her. She stood up and went to the window.

"Because, you know, he bit the guy he was fighting. Bit a part of his ear off."

"Really?" she said. "That's crazy."

"A little overkill, sure. He lost the fight."

July opened the curtains.

"If you turn off the lights in here, no one can see in," she said.

I didn't say anything, and she turned off the lights in the room and sat back down in front of me. The ambient light of the strip was just enough so I could see her outline. The air conditioner kicked on and I felt her hand on my knee.

"Can I make you comfortable?" she said.

"Yes," I said, and stood up. Her fingers fumbled with the button on my pants. I closed my eyes, but there were no visions. July could have been anyone in the darkness, but I knew what she was.

I smoked a Cohiba cigar on the back porch in 2008 and listened to my son Jaime tell his Iraq stories. He'd been stopping by more regularly in the past year since separating from the army and moving to Port Arthur, only two hours away. He wore his Chevron polo shirt and sipped a can of Bud Light. He looked good then, still fit and clean shaved, and I was glad to have him in my life.

Jaime's anger about Iraq had grown over his three deployments, and when he nearly took a sniper bullet during his final deployment and realized he couldn't explain what he was fighting for he got out at his first opportunity. Even so, sitting on my back porch, something came over him when he talked about his time in Iraq—an easy-to-access eagerness or melancholy that even he couldn't explain. I guessed he'd seen the worst of what the war brought having served in the roughest spots over there, but he always left out the graphic details even after I told him he could tell me anything.

I listened to his stories about shitty equipment, heat, and Robin Williams's and Drew Carey's USO shows. Stories about how you could buy a big screen television or get Popeye's Chicken on post. By then I was giving an honest attempt at pacifism, but I confess I wanted to hear the worst of what he saw. Sure, I wanted to help him work through any issues he may have been dealing with, but my offer wasn't entirely altruistic. I wanted to know how many people he had killed, and how, but my morbid curiosity only applied if they were clearly bad guys, which I knew wasn't the war he had fought in. I yearned to hear about his near misses and know if his rage against Rumsfeld and Cheney matched mine, but I never asked him directly about these things. Why? I'm not sure. Perhaps I was worried that he'd tell me the worst—maybe it was that he'd killed innocents, kids—and I wouldn't be able to say or do anything to help, or that I'd despise him in some way I couldn't control. I'd served in the military at a different time, fearing a different demise.

Jaime didn't have any plans for Halloween, so I asked him to stay over and help me hand out candy, which he accepted. He leaned back in the patio chair and surveyed my small backyard with its three Magnolia trees and a Tulane flag I flew during football season.

I didn't stop to consider it in 2008, but as I do now, I think of the thousands of miracles that had to take place to have him there on the back porch with me. Of all the places he could live, why Port Arthur? What compelled him to get in his car and drive two hours to come and sit with me? To say "yes" to handing out candy with his old man? Even though I'd made annual trips to see him in Alabama and had him out to my place a few times during his teenage years, I admit to not being there for him as much as he needed or wanted. But maybe it was enough. Maybe it was as simple as forgiveness or some emotional bond between father and son or the will of God. Maybe I was the only one that would listen to his war stories. It doesn't matter. Whatever it was he was there with me, his nose and chin my own and Alicia's smile.

"I got a good one about Mosul," he said.

"Yeah?"

"We couldn't win in Mosul. IEDs and small arms are fucking us everywhere, so we search houses and rough some people up all in the name of not dying, but you never find the right people or the stashes of guns and these people are eating or letting their kids take a goddamn nap and we're yanking them out of their houses, pissing them off. It's a shit way of doing things, but the city is full of assholes, so what do we do? Got to get them out of their houses so we can search. Well, we had a girl in our company that was hot as hell, a blonde. I'm telling you dad, hot as shit with this long blonde hair. So we head into Mosul and we stick this girl up on a Bradley and she took off her helmet and let that hair fall out. I come over the loudspeaker, 'Woman for sale! Woman for sale!' And what happens? Every fucking Iraqi dude is out there in about two seconds losing their fucking minds. Going crazy for our blonde, waving their arms and jumping up and down, and I say, 'Highest bid gets the woman! This beauty! Highest bid!' They're going apeshit, bidding everything they have, mules, goats, everything. I'm not kidding. These guys offering up their families. There was this one Iraqi, he must have been seven-feet tall, just freaking out. He was telling us to take his car, his house, you name it. I'll never forget him. Like freaky tall. They all wanted that blonde so damn bad, cause they don't have any, and I keep saying, 'Nope, not high enough. Not high enough,' whipping them up into a frenzy. The blonde is posing, whipping that hair around, running her fingers through it. Just taking it up a few notches. She must have been nervous, but you couldn't tell. And I'm on the loudspeaker, 'Higher! More! More!'

And while this is going on our guys are searching all of their homes. Silent as shit cause it's just the women home. Searched the whole neighborhood in twenty minutes and scored a mountain of guns and a few detonators without a single problem. No one shot at. No screaming. And when I get word from the LT we're done searching I tell the horny dudes, 'Sorry, the bids aren't high enough,' and we take off real quick. They were pissed, but no harm done. Even gave them a little thrill. We did this all over the place, and it worked every time."

Later that night, after the final trick-or-treaters, he turned to me. Something was wrong.

"Dad," he said. "I made up some stuff about that Mosul story."

"That's okay, son," I said. I meant it.

"There was no seven-footer. I don't know why I said that. Just stupid."

"It's fine."

"The rest of the stuff happened that like that, but…"

"Forget it."

A year and a half later Jaime sent me Dexter Filkins's *The Forever War*. I was shocked Jaime's Mosul scene was in there, described just as he'd said, minus the tall Iraqi. Filkins's version of the story noted that Jaime was reprimanded for the decision to put the blonde in such a vulnerable situation, something he never mentioned to me. Jaime inscribed the book, "Your famous auctioneer."

Jaime died of lung cancer not long after I received the book. It surprised all of us when the news came down, how far the cancer had progressed. Jaime's fellow soldiers claimed it was due to the burn pits on all the US bases over in Iraq, but it was impossible to prove. He moved back to

Birmingham for his final weeks to be close to Alicia, and I was by his side when he died on Alicia's living room couch. There's no moral in his death, not that I can find anyway. Alicia and I didn't reconcile in grief, although we did hug each other at the funeral, which means a lot to me.

Whenever I think of Jaime, I see him as an adult. That's my curse for not knowing him well enough as a child. Sometimes Jaime is on my back porch with a Bud Light. Sometimes he turns to me and tells me he made up a seven-foot-tall Iraqi. I confess I open *The Forever War* and read the part about the blonde. I can always find him in those two pages where no one gets killed.

Waiting for Red Dawn

I'm twelve, asleep in a room I've wallpapered with posters of NBA basketball players when my father shakes me awake, hands me a revolver, and whispers, "If something happens shoot for the body." I'm all heartbeat and dizzy in our narrow, dark, predawn hallway as I scoot forward, left hand on my father's back, right hand gripping this heavy gun—a loaded gun—and as we glide past my infant sister's bedroom I hear knocking. Someone's knocking on our front door, and everything jumbles together—*Shoot for the body, Murderer, Knocking, Are we shooting through the door? What criminal knocks? How big is a bullet?* And my father moves forward, disappears, so I crouch down on the floor in a flood of fear and close my eyes, then open them, but there's no difference in the darkness, and still this feverish knocking, and I wait for the shot, for my name in the night, and I feel the worn carpet on my feet, and I wait. The standoff's taking too long, and now a deep, slurring voice filters through the door, the deep voice hurls my father's name—*John*—and it comes to my ears in the same plead-scream my mother sang seconds after dumping boiling water on her feet. Then: lights on, door open, and our drunk neighbor spits out, *Your fucking backyard's on fire.*

Dawn arrives and I watch my father direct the small water stream from our garden hose onto a smoking pile of leaves we'd left for Glad Bags later that day. We'll never know what lit them, and I don't know why, but my father still grips his gun, and so do I. I feel small, but strong, like a half-trained sentinel. I look the silver gun over, and I see the brass backings of bullets waiting their turn. I decide to test the trigger and I do this slight tug and watch the revolver's hammer start its backward ride, but I stop early and everything slides back into potential. *Beautiful.* I do the tiny tug again, and the minuscule movement of the hammer intoxicates my limbs. My father shakes the morning cold out in his shorts and night shirt and old slippers and stares mesmerized at the water flow, intent on snuffing out our smoldering mound of natural debris, and for some reason, all at once, I realize that I could shoot him, right there. Not that I want to. It's that I could, with minimal effort, and I'd kill him if I aimed straight enough, and without prompt I stroke this strange rush of power and alarm that people must feel when they realize they can do absolutely anything they want if they have the nerve.

—

Growing up, my relatives would argue about which of them would be targeted first in a nuclear war. There was some sort of prestige to it all. An uncle in Colorado Springs claimed that NORAD would be the Russians' first target. "Mountain can't hold back a nuke." He was somehow proud of his proximity. My father said he would drive *toward* Colorado Springs because the "Rooskie's" technology was so poor, but somehow he argued our logging town of 1,500 near the California-Oregon border put us right in the USSR crosshairs. "There's an Army depot within a hundred miles." When an aunt brought up Fairfax, Virginia, everyone joked that the Soviets would want to keep the crooks in power, so DC would be spared, so they could argue and tax the cleanup workers.

⁓

If you ask most people what they fear now, how many would say nukes? My cousin called me after his last airline trip. There was a bearded, sturdy, Arab-looking man seated in front of him. My cousin had a confession: he knew the bearded gentleman was probably a saint, and my cousin watched him read a *People* magazine then sleep most of the way, but my cousin waged a war against his senses. He repeated to himself, *Don't smell for smoke. His shoes are shoes, not bombs. His shoes are shoes.* On the phone, he didn't ask me: "Am I a bad person?" What he asked was: "What does this mean?"

⁓

I'm twenty-six, teaching my wife Sarah how to throw the slide back on a Berretta 9mm pistol in the high desert outside of Albuquerque, New Mexico. It's taken me four years to convince her that we should own a gun and keep it in our home. This is the first time in her life she's touched a lethal weapon, and the slide proves problematic because you really have to crank it back in an odd pinch and pull motion, and her face snarls and her eyes narrow behind shooting glasses, and I know I have about fifteen seconds left before she gives up, makes me sell the gun, and refuses to broach the subject for the rest of her life. So I grab the handgun, ready it, and hand it back to her, handle first. After a deep breath, she rolls through the entire magazine of ammunition, and in the end she's punched a nice little bunching of holes in the human silhouette target twenty-feet away. She should be proud, and maybe she is, but she hands over the gun with head-tilt finality that tells me that I never need to ask her to prove her marksmanship again. On the ride back to our home she asks me again why we *need* a gun. I tell her all about home protection, intruders, and lethal force, the "don't mess with the Goolsbys" mountain upbringing I was privy to, the end-of-days scenario where we play out *Red Dawn*, and for levity, something about zombies. She doesn't challenge me, and it's a good thing, because I have no idea what the percentages are for home break-ins, not to mention Russian invasions.

Red Dawn premiered in 1984, and it gave people something else to fear besides Cold War nukes. In the film, Russian paratroopers land at a rural Colorado high school in the middle of history class. When the instructor attempts to confront the evil parachutists they greet him with AK-47 fire. In the resulting student scramble, a group of friends band together, raid a sporting goods store for survival necessities, and head for the mountains. Over the course of months, the small student group forms a resistance unit—they call themselves *Wolverines* and manage to wage an extremely successful and violent re-takeover of their small town where their parents sulk away in razor wire reeducation camps. At the time it was released, *Red*

Dawn was considered the most violent film by the *Guinness Book of Records* and The National Coalition on Television Violence, with a rate of 134 acts of violence per hour, or 2.23 per minute. Overall, the violence of the film didn't get to me. What I feared was that the Russians decided to start with some hick, rural town. Not New York. Not Los Angeles. They started with a town just like mine.

My history teacher was a bony, well-educated man scared of his own shadow. So what would happen? Would he let them walk right in and take care of business?

―――

I'm an English professor and an Air Force officer. I'm also in charge of the antiterrorism training at my school. It's an odd combination. I speak the virtues of Shakespeare, and I educate students and faculty on what to do if we have a shooter in our midst. Here are the answers: 1. Hide 2. Lacking an appropriate hiding place, do anything to survive.

―――

Tim, my best friend in high school, had a small cone-like lump of cartilage protruding from his neck. It was one of those odd biological missteps that you couldn't look away from once you noticed, not that it was incredibly obvious, except when Tim would embarrass and the party of rogue cells would go a shade whiter than the rest of him. One high school afternoon Tim was shot with a pellet gun by his younger brother. The pellet lodged 4mm away from his left eye, and left Tim in a hump in his living room, clutching his face as blood gushed onto the carpet. The ambulance came and Tim's brother was an emotional mess for a month. I was there the day Tim took off the bandages revealing a newly healed temple. I noticed his neck lump had disappeared. When asked, Tim replied, "The docs said it would go where it was needed."

—z—

In a hunting magazine I read a story about an 80-year-old woman in Southern Idaho, home alone, sucking on an oxygen mask wishing the seizures away, who pulls a .357 on a burglar and blasts him through the shoulder, then while he begs, puts another through his temple. The elderly woman suffered a broken wrist due to the recoil of the handgun. The write-up was under the section title: *Heroes in our Midst*.

—z—

I believed *Red Dawn*. In the winter of their resistance, two young men from the *Wolverines* deer hunt in the woods not far from their hideout. After knocking a decent buck dead they approach the animal and the seasoned hunter turns to the virgin, younger hunter.

"You drink the blood of your first," he says, and offers a mug. After minor bickering, the new killer raises the mug to his lips, gulps the still-warm blood, and smiles like the fluid is the one thing that has been missing from his life.

I killed my first deer while hunting with my father in the Jarbridge Wilderness in Northern Nevada. I was thirteen. We hadn't talked about *Red Dawn*, but it was with great trepidation that I approached the felled animal. My father was jovial, but I think he sensed my apprehension. He snapped a few photos while I held the deer's head off the ground. I managed to smile while I looked my father over for hidden cups, but there were none. When he mentioned dragging the buck back to the truck, all of a sudden I felt as if I would miss the blood milestone because he had forgot about the ritual, or perhaps he thought I wasn't up to it. Either way, I was simultaneously thrilled and disappointed, but something had to be said.

"When do, when do I drink blood?" I stuttered.

I'd confused him, and he opened his mouth, but nothing came out. When I mentioned where I'd absorbed the idea he simply shook his head.

He hadn't seen the film.

⟶

My father let my mom go deer hunting with him once, and he told me that husband/wife hunting would never happen again. She wouldn't slather the camo makeup on. She refused to sit still in the blind. And when a buck finally showed up, ready to be killed, my mother began to cry.

⟶

Every now and then we'd go practice shooting the variety of weapons my father kept: various gauges of shotguns, rifles, revolvers and pistols—one of which was "the kind James Bond uses." I enjoyed shooting up our spot in the woods. The explosions were vicious among the soft trees and their echoes rattled off the hills. My father's favorite gun was his Winchester .300 Magnum rifle. He'd always wait until dusk to shoot it because when the light faded enough you could see a fire glow spitting out with each blast.

Once, my mom was out with us, and my father must have dared her or promised her something, because she suddenly crouched, and using a stump as a brace, pointed the .300 Magnum at a painted paper plate. The gun roared and we all looked at the paper plate, holeless and mocking. When we glanced back to my mom the gun was on the bare ground—a sin in our family—and my father rushed over to pick it up, but instead, he stepped over the rifle and took my mom's face in his hands. It was then that I noticed she held her fingers to her right eye. Blood slid through the space between her fingers and raced down the backs of her hands. My father shouted to let him look, but she wouldn't unmask her eye. She wept while my father cussed and slapped his thighs then picked his favorite gun up out of the pine needles and dirt.

On the way back to town I know he wanted to tell her that you never put your eye right on the scope on account of the recoil. He was mad she needed stitches, and she was mad that she shot an elephant gun at a paper plate. They were in love, but wanted nothing to do with one another, and when we ran out of gas, my mom cussed for the first time in years and made my father stay with the 4Runner and my little sister as she and I walked the last three miles of dirt road together. She was quiet for a while—the bleeding had stopped—but she looked like she'd lost a one-punch fight. I wondered if the doctors would ask her what happened, all the while looking at my father's knuckles.

Mom was a valley girl at heart. She was a singer—a damn good one—and she starred in the local community chorus where my father reluctantly sang baritone. She'd made me take piano and trombone lessons, but I was about to quit them both for sports. The cold dusk settled around us, and in the distance logging trucks downshifted on the causeway into town. Our rutted road winded back and forth, and when I suggested a more direct route through the trees my mom ignored the proposal by humming. I recognized the melody and guessed its origins from one of my mother's favorite films: either *The Sound of Music* or that Streisand movie where she dresses like a Jewish man. She didn't look at me, but I guessed that she wanted me to sing along, so I did, softly, occasionally glancing at the now crescent bulge-cut where the hunting scope did its work.

When we reached the paved road I saw that we were dirty and my mom had wiped blood all over her arms and pants. We were zombie-like, wading out of the hills. I think of this bloodied image of my mom when I recall her answer to the "dream job" question.

"Broadway," she said. "Got the voice. Begging for the looks."

Later, after we'd hitched into town with a shell-shocked couple on their way to the coastal redwoods, my mom took a shower and got herself stitched up at the hospital before driving back out for my father and little sister. I didn't ask, but in the small Emergency waiting room where it took an hour to be seen she said, "If they get hungry out there, they've got guns."

~

I wonder if my children will fear the same things I fear.

~

I have a distant relative who owns three thousand acres in Nebraska. He farms alfalfa, soybeans, and the type of corn not meant for eating. He has a couple hundred head of cattle roaming the far reaches of his property. One summer we rode horses toward Wyoming. My crotch hurt on account of my lack of conditioning, and he could sense my unease.

"Let's hop off for a minute up here," he said.

Coming down off a plateau above a blooming wild-flower meadow we came across a concrete pad enclosed with fence. It was bizarre, this random square of fence out in the middle of nowhere. He didn't say anything right away although I had the impression he wanted to.

"Something special?" I asked.

"Nuke," he said, anxious to answer.

"What?"

"Nuclear," he said. "Bomb." He stroked his horse. "They lease the space."

Later, over lunch, I had the gumption to ask him how he felt about having a fueled-up, ready-to-go nuke on his property.

"I imagine it running out of fuel over the Pacific," he said. "Maybe it takes out Southern California. What would we lose? Hopefully, the ones we shoot will collide in midair with the ones the Russians shoot and give us the damndest fireworks show, and we all take a deep breath and agree to use swords."

The next day, we ran across coyotes in the distance. His rifle was up and he shot before I placed my hands over my ears.

We didn't ride over to the coyotes, but we did find a half-eaten calf.

"I wish they'd put more nukes out here," he said.

I thought about that. What do you say?

"I wish it was harder to kill," I said.

I'm proud of those words, but evil exists, and I often find reasons to take them back.

A remake of *Red Dawn* came out in 2012. This time it's Chinese paratroopers.

—⁊—

I own weapons: shotguns, rifles, handguns. They're locked up. In time I'll teach my children how to shoot them. I may give them the combination to the safe. If my wife asks me why they *need* to know how to shoot, I'll tell her it's a skill everyone should master. I don't know if "everyone" is the correct word, but I pray my children will be prepared to do more than hide and wait.

—⁊—

Fifteen years ago I bought some acreage in Southern Colorado outside Fort Garland. It's as rural as rural gets, around 9,000 feet up overlooking a yellow-grassed valley. On rare, clear days you can see three different mountain ranges holding snow in July. We go up there once or twice a year for a picnic, clean air, and let the kids get dirty. Guns and ATVs aren't allowed. My wife wants little to do with the parcel, and I understand. It's cold and windy for most of the year, and the elk we were promised upon purchase rarely settle within view. We bought it mainly for investment, but it hasn't valued over the years, and it's maybe even lost a bit. But she lets me keep it because she knows I relive my childhood among the aspen and pine and the horseflies that turn picnics into swatting wars. She knows I love to see my children negotiate an unpaved world that allows them to feel small and overwhelmed, yet filled with a joy they can't name. So that's all logical and aboveboard. What we don't talk about is my belief that this is the safest place to be if a nuclear war ever heats up. I don't bring up my depraved little fantasy where [insert evil country]'s parachutists fly in and take over our suburban paradise, and it happens to be a Saturday so we're all there at the house and we have 15 minutes to grab everything we need and get out, and we haul ass down to our sanctuary mountain land in Southern Colorado and unload the Honda and survey our mound of -50 degree sleeping bags, clothes, hand-pump flashlights, a solar radio, water, and dried food. We've said *Screw the rules*, and brought enough guns and ammo to give ourselves a nickname that'll stick. Our young children don't know any better, they don't know to be scared, so they play in the high mountain air while my wife and I set up camp during the warm season. That night, after the kids go down, the stars blast out like goddamn spotlights because we're so close, and we look around us, and, Jesus, if this isn't the best place you could be during an invasion.

So yes, I'm waiting for *Red Dawn*. And it would scare my wife, but that scenario sounds exciting to me in my twisted dream world where the invasion peters out after a week. Where I never have to raise my rifle and scope a target. Where no one ever gets hurt.

Hindu Kush

Jeannine, I think of you as I turn off *Super Why* and load
Carlos in the wagon and pull him to Kay Rees Park, the
park where wasps attacked us last summer by the stinking
water fountain and dying grass, where we can see the top of
downtown Salt Lake City; I think of you all morning and
relive last night, mid-Skype session, you in Afghanistan, in
your green flight suit, your brown hair pulled back, when
you asked me *how* I missed you, not *if* I missed you, but
before I could answer I heard the incoming mortar alarm
through my tiny computer speakers and watched you jump
away from the screen before the signal died; I pictured you
at Bagram Airfield in a metal coffin, quiet and still, and
later, a vision of you fingering the controls of your C-130,
alive and tired; I waited by the computer for a message to
arrive; I hit reload and reload and reload until one appeared
with no body, just the bolded subject line, *alive and fine i'll
call when I can :)*; this morning CNN scrolled a red ban-
ner: *Disaster in the Hindu Kush, Disaster in the Hindu Kush,
Disaster in the Hindu Kush,* and one of the commentators

said, "The killer of Hindus"; so I take Carlos to Feller Park
and watch him play in the mud, watch him eat mud, and
I think of you flying above the Hindu Kush, banking over
jagged peaks and tunnels and high desert, night-vision
goggles on, maybe a picture of me and Carlos tucked into
the instrument panel; you're saving lives or destroying
them, but I don't care which one it is anymore; your voice
plays all over me, your lie before you left, "Eight months
is nothing"; this slow crawl afternoon I wish away with
Sesame Street, Daniel Tiger, Bolt, and I hate you for signing
up for the Air Force, for thinking that you're defending
our country over there, for deploying when we could have
gotten pregnant again, for Skyping us and never crying;
I'm pissed that our yard is dead because Utah has dried
up, and I'm pissed that I'm the only father in group play-
dates contemplating yoga pants and *The Bachelor*; I wonder
where you are, right now—Asleep? Eating? Working out?
Ducking mortars? You could tell me anything and I'd believe you: you could tell me the time away has made you
love me more, that you're happier without me, that you've
found some Colonel and you're fucking him every spare
second; tonight, I scramble eggs Carlos refuses, even with
a promise of *Star Wars* if he eats, and he shouts "No," over
and over, so I slap him and fight the guilt as he melts down
and spills cold eggs all over the floor; I heap strawberry ice
cream on his plate and bask in his instant forgiveness; after
his bath I rub lotion on his cheek hoping the mark will be
gone by morning; you should know he rarely asks about
you, it's been days since he asked about you, but still, I tell
him you are okay, that there are only two months left till
he can hug you, but he doesn't seem to mind; he wants me
to answer questions about Jabba the Hut, if he can live on

land and in water, and if he can live in water, how long can he hold his breath? I wait for your phone call; you are alive, but I haven't heard your voice, and when I do, I'll cry, I'm sure of it; you asked me how I miss you, Jeannine; I day-dream and slap and stare at my inbox and laugh; I watch our son eat mud; tonight, I'm exhausted, and I wait for your voice; I eat a bowl of orange sorbet and listen for any trace of you; I hear the air breaks from the diesels out on I-80; I stare at my phone; a little after eleven I turn off the lights and put on our favorite porn, the one in a spaceship, but the moaning is just too much so I turn it off; I listen for the phone for minutes then I walk into your closet, find your red lingerie, and slide it on your pillow; I lean in close and hold your pillow to my chest; in the darkness I reach for my dick and smell the faintest whiff of your vanilla perfume.

Waist Deep at Hapuna

I was sixteen, newly licensed, and I couldn't fool the cop after five shots of Black Bear whiskey, so why try? By the time mom picked me up at the Hilo jail, I was mostly sober and unafraid. It wasn't the first time I'd been there. As a kid you're always told that jail is the worst place on earth, but that isn't true, not by a longshot. Google Alzheimer's or Jaycee Dugard.

Mom wore a *Fuck Cancer* T-shirt and a misaligned wig. She'd named me after herself, so when the deputy called out "Marie" we both said, "What?" We drove home listening to the Deftones album I loved. I didn't know if she had the strength to lecture or beat me, so I paid my respect by staying quiet as we passed over the Wailuku River. Our empty driveway shouldn't have surprised me, but it did, just as it had for the year since dad left for the hellhole that is Las Vegas. Later, as I showered, I wondered if I would have to live with him and his fat girlfriend if mom died before my eighteenth birthday, but I knew there was a good chance no one would care where I went.

Way too early that morning mom came into my bedroom and turned on the lights. She wasn't impulsive, so it scared the crap out of me. She wore her UNLV shorts from her old days, and she made me look at the new scars where her breasts used to be. She held a white belt in her hand, and she stood there for five minutes, her arms at her sides. I thought she would hit me or make me touch her, so I cowered and begged her to go away.

"Do you want to look like this?" she said.

"No," I said.

"This is where you're headed."

I was afraid and confused, and why not? When I glanced at the motionless ceiling fan mom said, "No. Here," and pointed at her chest.

Her scars looked like pink smiles, and I could see purple veins through her skin. The color had drained from her face, and she looked down at herself and grimaced. Her legs were long and toned because she worked out like crazy through chemo, as if she was still her eighteen-year-old volleyball player self. Fanaticism, maybe, but it's better than daytime soap operas and a liter of Coke. But mom's upper half? It was no longer hers, at least that's what I read in her horror.

"You drink again and I'll kill you," she said. She was still staring at her body. If it had been any other time or place I would have laughed. Mom never carried through with threats. That's what I hated about her.

Before she turned and left she said our name, but how was I to know if she was talking to me?

Although I didn't think about it that morning, I've often wondered if you can recover from genuine loneliness, and each time I convince myself that the answer is yes.

Sure, I've seen sane people jump from the Golden Gate. I've heard stories about one-legged vets hanging themselves in closets, or people catching Alzheimer's in their forties. I've put down a pint of Black Bear on a Tuesday night, all alone. All of it is horrible shit, but I remember the Monday my dad's Jeep returned to our driveway in Hilo. He came through the door with fried chicken and sat down like it was nothing. I've waded into the calm ocean at Hapuna with mom and held her weightless body in my arms. I've seen her yellow bikini stuck to her flat chest, how the whole damn beach noticed. Fuck them and their pathetic whispers. Mom walked me down the goddamn aisle, and you still think there's sanctity in our bodies?

Acceleration Hours

"String of Pearls."
"I've Found Someone."
"Rainy Days and Mondays."
"If You Could Read My Mind."

The old people in Wishwell Retirement Home call out to the bearded, overweight, twenty-five-year-old man they've nicknamed Steinway, although his evening singing sessions take place on a cheap Casio keyboard the home's services director bought at Target for a hundred bucks. They want melody.

Steinway. The name doesn't faze Trevor Gatlin. In fact, even after several months of these gigs he still enjoys *becoming* Steinway, a more intense, mostly energetic, caring version of Trevor for these evening sessions, and why not? The pay is good ($20/hr.), and the twelve octogenarians that show seem pretty damn happy as he rolls through his standard, no-longer-bizarre sampling of Beethoven, Glenn Miller, Gordon Lightfoot, Carpenters, Michael Jackson, and Cher.

In between songs Steinway enjoys a massive, evenly mixed gin and tonic he squeezes out of a plastic *Lassen Volcanic National Park* water bottle. He's learned over the months that being a bit buzzed by the end of the performance is a necessity ever since Mr. Nowak's family began paying Steinway under the table to stick around after the singing and listen to a war story or two before bedtime.

Nowak likes to memory stroll across the gore of Guadalcanal: how his buddy's blown off foot landed in his arms, the one about shooting a Japanese soldier in the chest then giving the guy a cigarette just before he died in the dark sand, how Nowak almost had his dick bitten off by a small shark when swimming in the ocean after the battle was over, the time he finally got to use the flamethrower on the Japanese tunnels and ended up losing his left ear.

Steinway knows it will probably be one of these stories as he butchers the chorus of his final song of the evening, the oft-requested Jackson's "Man in the Mirror," but Steinway isn't concerned or hurried, it's not as if he has somewhere else to be by the 8:30 p.m. bedtime—he works the day shift at the Chevron gas station—and after all, the extra $30 a night from Nowak's family helps pay for the occasional trip to Reno with Rashad or a steak and pitcher of Miller Light at the Ranch House, as well as the fact that Nowak has proven himself a kind, if opinionated soul—always asking Steinway if he's comfortable while he listens in the creaking rocking chair by Nowak's bed, offering Steinway an occasional sip of his chamomile tea, trashing President Obama—and there's something Steinway appreciates about Nowak's vitality. Unlike many others in the home, death's call doesn't appear imminent for the tan, clear-eyed Nowak. He walks without aid, knows which decade he's in, jokes about midnight escapes, and recently shouted out "Eminem" during one of Steinway's performances.

And sure, Nowak has his moments, nights when he rails against the overpowering Lysol smell of the home, feeling trapped with the "hanger-oners," a term he brings forth on weeks when there's been more than one Wishwell death, and more rare evenings when he prefers to listen to Steinway talk about his life, which, if buzzed enough, Steinway will grant, typically self-censoring himself to his (Trevor's) love of music, beer, and a deteriorating desire to finish up at Lassen Community College. Off limits: vulnerability, elation, Steinway's boyfriend Rashad, and Steinway's recent, deep-seated fear that Rashad will soon end things.

But most nights there's Nowak's war stories, always delivered with a non-apologetic tenor which Steinway finds fascinating, welcoming, with none of the modern-day PTSD woe-is-me crap he loathes. If he had to choose a favorite narrative, Steinway would select the Japanese soldier-cigarette story. With some recent encouragement from Steinway, Nowak has mined deeper into the specifics, to the point that Steinway has noticed that Nowak switches the brand of the cigarette the soldier bums then smokes before he dies, a small, seemingly insignificant detail that portends memory loss or active imagination, either one a worthwhile if minor excitement in the bowels of Wishwell.

This Wednesday night Steinway has gone relatively easy on the gin and tonic and he accepts a sip of Nowak's tea after he sits down in the bedroom rocking chair with a grimace. It's 7:37 p.m. and Steinway feels the familiar aches run through his chest and right arm.

Nowak's room is decorated with photographs and drawings of whales, except for two small photos of Grace Kelly and Farrah Fawcett on his bedside table. Nowak is still in his day clothes—Eddie Bauer yellow polo shirt and khakis.

"I'm not tired," Nowak says. "Is this the night we break out?"

"Sure," Steinway says and taps his chest.

"You're still alive."

"You make a fatty sing and this is what you get." Steinway grabs his belly. "A few Tums and I'll live till a hundred." He's always joked through the embarrassment.

"They got new pills to help with that."

"Sure, you have an extra ten grand you want to give me?" Steinway says.

"Damn, Obama." Nowak smiles. "Why don't you put some water in that bottle of yours? That'll kick twenty, thirty pounds."

"It's mostly water," Steinway says, annoyed at the unsolicited weight-loss advice.

"Tonic."

"Water," Steinway says. "Tell me something new. I'm tired of the shark shit. I know it's not going to bite you. Although it gets *really* close." Steinway brings his hands to his cheeks. "Oh. My. It almost bit you. But. It. Didn't."

"I don't feel like talking. I feel like walking. Need some air. And you do too. They just cleaned the damn place. Lysol everywhere. Can you smell it?"

"Sure."

"No, you don't. You can't smell anything. There's such a thing as too clean. You can't clean outside."

"That's not true," Steinway says and stares down a painting of two humpback whales breaching the ocean. "Raking leaves from the lawn, trimming trees..."

"You're in a mood. Jesus, let's go."

"Fine," Steinway says, and rises with a grunt.

Outside on the large concrete patio Nowak leans against the building. They've been quiet for a few minutes, listening to the small town night sounds. The fresh air has helped them both.

"Tired of the shark story, huh?"

"That was mean," Steinway says. "But you still got your dick. The shark doesn't get you. When you know the ending there's only so many times..."

"You get your thirty bucks for listening."

"Don't get salty, old man," Steinway says, purposefully adding a subtle tone of endearment. He does value the extra thirty bucks, but tonight he's noticeably sluggish and wishes Nowak's bedtime would rush forward.

"After a while they brought dogs in for the caves. How about that, Steinway? You like dogs? You want a dog story?"

"Sure," Steinway says.

"How many guys you gonna lose before you try other means? The flamethrowers were running out of juice. Try resupplying in the middle of the Pacific. So we'd send the dogs in first. And they'd do fine. A couple got shot up, stabbed. Nobody cared. Our guys were dying in those tunnels. You can imagine."

"How do you get dogs to Guadalcanal?" Steinway says, genuinely interested. He's never considered dogs on ships or airplanes on the way to battle. None of his infrequent interactions with war films or books have included dogs. How do you keep them quiet? Do you need to?

"That's a stupid question," Nowak says. "Here's the right question. How do you get dogs to know the difference between Americans and Japs?"

"Well?" Steinway says.

"You don't. That's the key. You just train them to get angry at everything besides their handler. That's why you send them in the tunnels first. They'd just as soon attack one of ours. It happened more than once."

"How do you get them angry at everything?"

"Plus, it's dark as hell in the tunnels."

"But how do you get them angry?" Steinway says.

"Fight them against one another for starters. But not too much. Can't have them injured, but that's what the handlers told us. Stateside they fight them against one another before shipping them over."

"Michael Vick shit," Steinway says.

"Who?"

"Football player. Got caught fighting dogs."

"They do that in the south, you know."

"That was his defense," Steinway says, "how he was raised or something. Pit Bulls or Rots, I forget. Doesn't really matter. He was treated like a child murderer. Sent to jail. Kicked out of the league."

"Must not have been much going on in the world if people went nuts over dogfighting. Was there nothing else to get worked up about? A couple dogs fighting. Jesus."

"You tell me," Steinway says. "The Vick thing wasn't that long ago. There's always a lot to get worked up about. Take your pick."

"You interrupted my dog story."

"Does it get better than 'We sent them into the tunnels first'?"

Nowak shakes his head and fingers the lowest button on his polo.

"Not much gets your attention. You're a downer. Aren't you supposed to be keeping me alive?"

"I'm supposed to listen. That's what your loving family says."

"Loving family," Nowak repeats. "I need a cigarette. I don't care if they visit. I'm happy here. Everyone wants to feel sorry for me. Why?"

"I don't feel sorry for you," Steinway says.

"Good."

Steinway checks his watch: 7:48.

"Let's go to Chevron," Nowak says. "You're still working there?"

Steinway sees the wonder in Nowak's face. This isn't a throwaway request. And while Steinway isn't ashamed about his employment, he has never been quick to volunteer the Chevron information to people he meets. Even the kindhearted, like his boyfriend Rashad, initially give the head-tilt, pity smirk he despises. But there's enough dignity in him to speak clearly when he eventually says "Chevron." He could be collecting unemployment checks like a few of the uninjured losers he knows.

"You know I am," Steinway says. "What about it?"

"Let's go."

"You got forty minutes until bedtime, Nowak. It'd take ten to sign you out."

"I'll give you an extra twenty bucks."

"A hundred," Steinway says.

Nowak pulls out a fat leather wallet from his front pocket and fishes out two twenties and hands them over.

"Congrats, now you can afford Tanqueray," Nowak says.

By the time they hit Main Street Steinway senses a chill although it's still in the sixties. The shiver might be the nerves that open up inside him. If caught, there will be insignificant consequences, perhaps a throwaway lecture from Wishwell's manager, and Steinway tries to laugh off the imagined scene, but he's unsuccessful. The pain in his chest hasn't subsided, which isn't all that unusual. Still, he's not interested in prolonging this experience. The effects of the gin and tonic have long retreated, and the acuity of the night excursion doesn't bring him anything but responsibility, something he didn't anticipate and desire when he finished his set earlier that night.

The county has recently put in sidewalks, an improvement the lumber mill town greeted with ambivalence, but Nowak is giddy, saying the names of the stores they pass: "Holiday Market," "Antlers Motel," "Kopper Kettle."

It's only a quarter mile to the Chevron, but seems much longer to Steinway at their slow pace.

"Knotbumper. Bank of America."

"You're not in prison, Nowak." Steinway says. "You never get out?"

"I gave you forty bucks for a stroll. What do you think? I'm not paying to hold your hand."

Steinway attempts a breath before his reply but his body revolts into a coughing fit.

"You okay?"

"Fine," Steinway says, recovering.

"We're not going back."

"I'm fine," Steinway says, and he believes it. He's lived with his body long enough.

"You're not sweating are you?"

"I'm not dying, if that's what you mean," Steinway says. "No CPR tonight, Nowak. Don't get your hopes up."

"You can read my mind. How did you know? Nothing more I want than to pump on that chest."

"You'll go before me," Steinway says. "Count on it."

"You're a bunch of fun, you know that? You should be paying me."

The Chevron station is empty, save for Sheryl, who works the register. She's a little older than Steinway and wears two dreamcatcher earrings that almost touch her shoulders. She chews Skoal Longcut, the same as Steinway. They are friendly at shift change and Steinway remains in her debt for introducing him to his boyfriend Rashad. Still, Steinway often senses some ill-defined skepticism whenever she looks directly at him.

"Can't get enough?" she says to Steinway as the men enter the mini-mart.

Steinway nods at her.

"Go crazy, Nowak," Steinway says. "You got five minutes."

"I got all night. Still got free will, buddy."

Nowak starts down the aisle of jerky and candy. A country radio station is at commercial: used cars over in Susanville.

Steinway leans on the checkout counter and Sheryl nods at Nowak.

"Dude from Wishwell," Steinway says. "Ex-Marine needed a walk."

"Of all places to go."

"His choice," Steinway says and puts his hand out. "Save me." Sheryl opens the can of Skoal and he takes a pinch, the smell familiar and glorious. He slides the dip in with a practiced touch. Steinway started chewing at fifteen and continued even after being forced to look at multiple photographs of cancerous inner lips in the high school nurse's office—infected white and cavernous. The images haunt him occasionally, but whenever he flips his lip over in his bathroom he only sees the pink hue of health.

Near the back of the store Nowak inspects a massive, four dollar bag of Swedish Fish.

"He's missing an ear," Sheryl says. "That's not great to look at."

"Flamethrower accident from the war," Steinway says. "That's what he claims."

"But it's so...clean."

"It's been seventy years or whatever," Steinway says.

"What war?"

"World War II."

Sheryl raises her eyebrows, but doesn't speak.

"What?" Steinway says.

"Nothing."

"Anything exciting?" Steinway says.

"Meth head almost got hit on his bike a few minutes ago. That got my attention. I just heard the tires."

"Too bad the guy missed," Steinway says.

"It was a F-150. Would have been over quick. Meth head barely even noticed. He was on some pink BMX bike. I've never seen him, but I'm sure he'll be in here sooner than later. Hopefully your shift."

"If it hit him square he'd be dead." The voice is Nowak's, who Steinway had briefly forgotten. Nowak holds an open can of Bud Light.

"What are you doing?" Steinway says.

"I'll drink it outside."

Nowak puts a five dollar bill on the counter.

"You can't drink it outside," Steinway says. "Where do you think you are?"

"This is interesting," Sheryl says. "Let him stay. Who cares? No one's around."

"Sheryl," Steinway says.

"You Mr. Rules now?" Sheryl says. "I do inventory on the lottery tickets."

"Jesus," Steinway says. "Don't do that." Stunned, he brings his hands to his chest. "What? Sheryl." His vision blurs on the periphery, but his eyes lock on the plastic case that houses the various lottery tickets. It's been a year since he started lifting one 7-7-7 scratcher a week, and he's grown comfortable with the trifling thievery. He once won $500, which he cashed down in Chico.

"And you're a Marine, right?" Sheryl says to Nowak.

"Guadalcanal," Nowak says and points to where his left ear should be. "Lost it over there." He takes a few gulps of the beer.

"Sheryl," Steinway says, ready to plead.

"Forget it," Sheryl says without a glance his way. To Nowak: "My grandpa was on Iwo Jima. It's funny. You always hear about these greatest generation guys coming home who wouldn't talk about it. Some quiet hero crap or something. But my grandfather told war stories all the time. Couldn't get him to shut up about how rough it was."

"This guy, he's a talker, a lot, too," Steinway says, stumbling back into the conversation, but still shaken from Sheryl's lottery ticket comment and subsequent "Forget it." Steinway looks at her and she appears calm, like nothing has happened—no accusation at all—but Steinway can't slow his heart, and the shooting pain in his arm returns.

"We've got to go," Steinway says.

"Where?" Nowak says.

"Damn it," Steinway says. "It's time."

"You got a good story for me?" Sheryl says. "Nowak, is it?"

"Yes."

"You can see we're not expecting a big crowd tonight."

"Seriously, we have to go," Steinway says. He's impatient and he's dying, only slowly and unaware. The final heart attack won't arrive until the following night when he sits alone on the shore of Lake Almanor.

"Sure," Nowak says then finishes his beer. He walks to the back of the store and grabs another, opens it, drinks, and comes back to the counter. "I gave you five bucks, right?"

"You're fine," Sheryl says. "Tell me about the ear. Flamethrower, right?"

"Steinway tell you that?"

"You mean Trevor?" she says. "Sure."

"He's been listening to me although he pretends not to," Nowak says.

"Nowak, you're on your own," Steinway says. He hands Nowak back the two twenties. "I got nothing to do with you. You hear me? You walked away on your own."

"Relax," Sheryl says. "I've never seen you this pissed."

"I'm fine, for the thousandth time," Steinway says. "I don't..." He catches his breath. "Want nothing to do with this guy. Too much."

"It's just Wishwell, Trevor," Sheryl says. "They don't care."

Steinway can't will his body to leave the Chevron. He considers calling Rashad, but he decides to wait until the pain subsides.

"So, these flamethrowers," Nowak says. "First, you'd have to rub on this protection cream before you went out. All over your face. You knew it was only a matter of time before you got burned a little. You're shooting the damn thing in these caves. Not a lot of places for the fire to go. And it's liquid fire, not just a flame. Not a lot of people know that. We'd get excited as hell. Nothing like it. We get all pumped up. We got 'em cornered and we're scared, but mainly excited. It's hard to explain. You're so damn tired, but ready to go. Hyper. Everything's going so fast and slow at the same time."

"Acceleration seconds," Sheryl says. "That what my grandpa called it. You get so excited and crazy that time speeds up instead of slowing down. But you stay in control somehow."

"Hell, I'm talking about acceleration *hours*," Nowak says in between drinks. "You think people die quick in the caves? Hell, no. You got to keep your wits. It takes time to die. You got to speed things up to get through the day."

"And your ear? Short version," Sheryl says. "Trevor isn't crazy. You need to get back."

"So the Japs are in the caves, and they won't come out. Captain gives the order to fire up the cave, so I do, and I get 'em. But the screams. It's a hell of a thing, even when you want to kill."

Steinway escapes from the pain long enough to text Rashad.

Trevor: Come pick me up at the Chevron. Explain later

Rashad: You ok? Why at Chevron?

Trevor: Just come get me. Messed up

Rashad: On way.

It'll take Rashad ten minutes to arrive.

"Your ear," Sheryl says. "Tell me about your ear."

"I got too close to the flame," Nowak says. "That's the short version."

Sheryl looks at Steinway.

"Nothing to do with him," Steinway says. "He knows the way back."

"I know the way back," Nowak says. "Bedtime for war hero. Yes?" He straightens up, leaves the half-drunk can on the counter, and turns to go. "Thanks, Steinway. Maybe mix the songs up a bit tomorrow night."

"Fuck you," Steinway says.

Nowak walks through the doors, then looks back and points at Steinway and winks.

"That guy is full of shit," Sheryl says after Nowak disappears into the darkness past gas pump #4.

"What?"

"He was never in World War II. Are you kidding me? He's too young. What's he, sixty, sixty-five?"

"How the hell am I supposed to know?" Steinway says.

"You're the one bringing him in here. And there weren't any flamethrowers, Trevor. The guy is screwing with you."

Steinway goes silent trying to piece together everything. On the radio, George Strait's "Ocean Front Property," and Sheryl starts to hum along. Steinway sees the self-important know-it-all pride she radiates.

"Don't worry about the lottery tickets," Sheryl says. "I don't know why I said that."

"Sure," Steinway says. "Okay." He's relieved, but only slightly. Her accusation arrived so quickly, so out of the blue.

"I've been fighting with Bill," Sheryl says.

Steinway hears her, but doesn't reply. He lifts his recovering arm, shakes it out, and finishes with a small wave goodbye.

Steinway walks down Willow Way and turns south on First Avenue, guessing Rashad is driving the back way to Chevron, but Steinway is wrong, which will earn him an extra five minutes of solitude and Rashad's fleeting scorn.

Finally alone, Steinway gives into the solitude of the moment and attempts to corral his thoughts. Rashad will find him soon and demand an apology then immediate optimism, a reoccurring sequence from Rashad at the conclusion of every one of their arguments. Steinway simultaneously loves and loathes it.

The night has cooled and Steinway wonders if Nowak found his way back, although it's an absurd notion that anyone could get lost in this town. Nowak is probably crawling into bed or already asleep, Grace and Farrah smiling nearby. He'll probably live forever, no matter if he's sixty or eighty years old, an earless wonder, damn him.

Steinway is scheduled to perform the following night at Wishwell, but he decides right then to skip the performance and head out to the West Shore of Lake Almanor tomorrow. He could use a break from the Lysol, Nowak, and Cher. They'll forgive him immediately when he shows up on Friday night. He knows that.

Soon, the low beams of Rashad's Honda Accord blind Steinway and he hears Rashad's voice through the open window before he's come to a stop.

"You told me Chevron, goddammit. What's wrong with you? Why aren't you at Wishwell? Sheryl says you were with some crazy dude. Trevor, are you listening to me?"

The car smells like marijuana and Rashad drives under the speed limit, which means he's stressed. After a sincere apology and a quick rundown of the evening's events, Steinway reaches over and holds Rashad's hand, and Rashad squeezes. Rashad wears the gold Rolex Steinway bought him after cashing the winning scratcher ticket.

"I'm here," Rashad says. "That's what matters. We're here together."

Rashad's voice has always calmed Steinway, and it works its magic again tonight—his beautiful reassurance, the enchantment of "together." Steinway closes his eyes and leans his head back onto the headrest. No pain. No responsibility. It's these moments of peace he'd love to slow down to a crawl, just let them flow over him and back again, but he finds it's always the opposite of his wish: the speed at which they'll soon be home (hopefully Rashad stays the night), the blink of an eye until morning, and with it, the Chevron cash register. But it's fine. He's fine. Yes, he'll skip Wishwell tomorrow. The West Shore will be deserted this time of year. He can go out there and throw rocks into the lake and watch the sun go down behind Mount Lassen.

"Bublé," Rashad says, and turns up "Haven't Met You Yet" on the car's stereo. "Ah, Michael, sing to me."

Rashad's one-person-I'd-run-away-with crush, Michael Bublé, croons his hit, and Steinway's hands reach out in front of him and begin to play the imaginary piano keys positioned there.

"You can play this song?" Rashad says. "Amazing. You can play the shit out of it, can't you? You know how rare that is? You know that? Say you're amazing. Say it. Open your eyes and look at me. You hear me? Say you're amazing."

Why I Listen to
My Children Breathe

Halfway through my vasectomy I look down to see the wide-eyed intern whom I agreed could *watch* the proceedings poke something into my groin and say, "Oops." The lead doctor, a calm, motherly presence up to this point, purses her lips and whispers loud enough for me to hear, "You never say 'Oops.' Never."

I grimace and clench my hands.

I hear the slow tick of some hidden clock.

The doc's words don't seem to bother my wife Sarah and my squirming one-year-old daughter, Abby. Against my initial protest, they're sitting inches from my left shoulder, because, as my wife put it, "You watch me push kids out, I watch you get snipped." They glance around the room with the calm faces of the unsliced.

This scene occurs in a tiny "minor surgery" space in the bowels of the Pentagon, performed by a doctor and intern that, by military and legal rules, cannot be sued for malpractice, no matter the error. As an Air Force officer, I normally work a couple floors above the room where I now lie, legs spread-eagled. Every other day in the building, I wear a uniform of dark blue dress pants, a freshly ironed buttoned-up light blue shirt, dark blue tie, and an assortment of badges, but at this moment I sport only a green North Face T-shirt, white ankle socks, and a recently shaved groin.

Smiling at me with a practiced *I've-seen-worse* look, the doc says, "Everything's just fine." I want to believe her, but I hear the intern's loud breathing. Over by a row of blue cabinets, he stares at his fingers.

Suddenly, I realize I should have asked more questions when the doc said that knocking me out wasn't an option on account of this only being "minor surgery." For a split second I consider slamming my head on the table. With enough force, I might buy myself a couple minutes, reprieve from this world-class awkwardness.

I recall the seemingly well-rationalized "Are we done having kids/who gets the operation?" rundown with Sarah: we have all the kids we want (three); they're healthy; the operation is easier, safer for the man; it shouldn't hurt at all; this particular doc has performed thousands of these ops; it's free while we're in the military. I didn't offer any counterarguments, only a pause to remember that my mom was the one who had her tubes tied after my brother Jacob and I were born, and to wonder if she regretted that decision.

I peek over at Abby, her Disney-sized blue eyes and four teeth. I reach my hand out to her. I don't know what I'm searching for exactly, perhaps a brief respite from the nightmare moment, to acknowledge the power of progeny, of unconditional love, but she begins to fuss and slaps my hand away.

My breathing quickens and the white operating room flexes and narrows. For the first time I realize there is no ambient noise, nothing to cover up the sound of little metal tools hitting the tray, tennis shoe squeaks, a whisper to a first-time intern. All of my other operations had music: right hip in '95—The Rolling Stones' "Honky Tonk Woman"; left foot in '99—U2's "Mysterious Ways"; and, memorably, just before going under in '02 for my wisdom teeth, a vision of my surgeon nodding his head to Dr. Dre's "Nuthin but a 'G' Thang." But here, vas deferens in '13— nothing.

Up to this point, although uncomfortable, there hasn't been much acute pain to note, more of a weird expectation of pain combined with never-before-felt internal pressure; perhaps even a tentative acknowledgement that it *should* hurt when someone takes a scalpel to my nerve-bundled testicles; also, the mental weight of knowing I'm voluntarily doing this to myself. Still, I can request another numbing shot to my groin if any of this is too much, but I would be asking for an additional shot to my groin. I consider asking for the shot in the abstract only.

Despite my best intentions, for the remainder of the operation I can't keep my body from jerking every time I feel the slightest pinch or pull. I had been a relative statue up to the "Oops" moment, and the doctor grows annoyed with my newly discovered gyrations during the cauterizing phase of our dance. She keeps saying, "That shouldn't hurt," but offers no options.

The cauterizing machine makes a beep about two seconds before each hot pulse to my testicles, and after a couple of jolts I fight the battle of my life in repeating two-second increments. I close my eyes and beg my body to calm down, to forget the timing, to think of a white beach, the Rocky Mountains in autumn, anything to take me away from here. It's in this pleading moment that my devil mind flashes me an image of a naked Rebecca De Mornay in *Risky Business* (blonde, healthy, Nordic-looking goddess), the effect of which triggers some sort of apocalyptic irony/coincidence/confusion mash-up within my now melting brain and body-rushing blood. Simultaneously, I fear the cauterizing pain and the possibility of a mid-operation erection. Amidst the chaos I open my eyes and tilt my head up to make sure my taped-to-my-belly penis is still there. It is. Small and scared, thank God.

Then, I hear the cauterizing machine beep—*one Mississippi, two Mississippi*—and I feel my hips and butt tense and lift as the machine pulses me with fire.

"That doesn't help," the doc says.

Finally, an hour after walking into the room on not enough Valium, I'm all sewed up and lightheaded, starting to find my legs. I carefully step into a gauze diaper. I'm offered a wheelchair, which I accept. They all appear surprised. Apparently, most men walk out on their own. But I don't care. I'm way past pride.

Once seated, I'm told to masturbate as soon as I'm ready.

"But I can wait a few days, right?"

"You'll know when you're ready, but don't wait too long."

My chest tightens.

The doc adds, "You'll need to masturbate at least twenty times in the next month and a half." She hands me a clear, plastic cup with lid. "Bring a sample in at the end to make sure there's no more swimmers."

I cringe and place my hands on the top of my head.

The doc throws me a tired, half-smile.

"Sorry for the twitching," I say. "Just not used to sharp things near that area I guess."

It's an earnest offering because I do feel bad about moving around so much. Still, I can't be the only twitcher she's encountered in her line of business.

"Yep," the doc says.

Sarah stands up with Abby and thanks everyone. The intern cleans something in the sink and keeps his back to us. I wait for him to turn around, but a new silence lingers long enough to signal our exit, so we start for the door.

"You know," says the doctor, reaching for Sarah's shoulder and nodding at me. "He's the type of person that would faint in a bear attack. The bear would eat him."

We wait for the doctor to laugh, but there's nothing. No tonal meanness or levity or smirk or head nod or pat on the back or middle finger.

"Oh," Sarah says.

—✎—

Fifteen minutes later on the way home, I ride shotgun and pray for smooth roads in our Honda Pilot as Sarah weaves in and out of Washington, DC, traffic. Our daughter naps in her car seat.

"Did she say a bear would fucking eat me?" I ask.

"She said you would faint."

"Who says that?"

"She just meant the twitching, I think. Maybe being lightheaded. Who cares?"

"I wouldn't faint." I say. "I'd fight back. Shit, I'd try. I'd jam a stick in its eye or kick or something. I wouldn't just fall down unconscious."

There's a traffic jam over the Potomac River and Sarah slows the car to a stop. She looks over at me.

"I know you would. Relax. Besides, aren't you supposed to ball up?"

"What does she know about bears?" I say. "I grew up around bears. Bears don't even like to eat people. Black bears a little. Grizzlies will kill you, but don't eat you. Does she know that? And I don't know of anyone who faints. Fainting isn't even on the table for reactions. And she tells me that after her intern welds my testicle in the wrong place. Shouldn't I get jumpy? Does she just want me to lie there and let them Picasso my shit?"

"But you're supposed to ball up so they play with you instead of kill you. I've heard that."

"There's a big damn difference between fainting and purposely balling up on the ground. If you ball up on the ground and the bear starts to eat you then you can fight for your life and stab it in the eye. But if you've fainted, you aren't in a ball and it can just eat you. If it wants to eat you, which it doesn't."

"You'd wake up," she says.

"Do you know what unconscious means?"

A police car edges by with lights on, but no siren.

"Why do you keep saying stab it in the eye?" my wife says. "The bear will be moving around. It's not going to stand still and let you find a stick and stab it."

"Jesus, I mean do anything to live. Stabbing it in the eye seems like it would hurt."

"There might not be a stick nearby."

"You can use your finger, whatever. If you're fighting a bear you are probably going to lose anyway. But our brilliant doctor doesn't know that it most likely won't eat you."

"If you're dead who cares if it eats you?"

We move, but only a car length.

"The bottom line is I wouldn't faint."

"I don't think you'd faint."

"Thanks."

—✐—

I'm a fourteen-year-old Mormon kid who has never masturbated, and our family gets this free six-month HBO trial at our house, so I start staying up late. It's 1992, and my buddies tell me Cinemax has the good soft-core stuff, but still, I hold out hope HBO will bless me with at least partial nudity. One night, *Risky Business* is on. Everyone's asleep; still, I thumb the volume down. As Tom Cruise starts fondling Rebecca De Mornay on screen, I feel myself go hard and debate ending my self-love celibacy. I don't know if there's actual no-masturbation doctrine anywhere in the Bible or Book of Mormon, but there's enough context clues in Sunday school to guess that God would be pretty upset at a young man jobbing himself a few hours before taking the sacrament. But still, I'm teenaged, and De Mornay is ungodly hot, and I think I might come even if I don't touch myself. I wonder if there's a concession between release and salvation somewhere in the night, and within ten seconds I think I've found a compromise as I grab my penis but don't move my hand. *If something happens*, I think, *then it happens.*

I feel myself hard and pulsing. I let the pressure build and overtake me as De Mornay straddles young Cruise, smartly sliding up and down, up and down, and I think

I may suffocate, but I manage to breathe. I consider dry humping the new couch, and I hate myself and absolve myself: I didn't seek out the I-want-to-do-this-beautiful-woman-all-night-long urge but here it is, undeniable and strong. And yet, this sensation collides with the vision of a white robed, muscular, Caucasian God, looking down, shaking his head, shaking a tiny bottle of White Out, taking out the little White Out brush and painting over "Jesse Goolsby" on the "Welcome to Heaven" list. And then, too quickly for me and my racing insides, the sex scene ends, and fully clothed actors talk on screen in daylight and my blood slowly settles and a dull ache ebbs forth from my testicles. I think about how I'll be okay if I'm asked to say a prayer in front of people in ten hours. I'm still clean.

Sir Astley Cooper performed the first vasectomy in 1823 on a dog.

My childhood dog's name was Nephi—a golden retriever named after one of the leading prophets in the Book of Mormon. According to scripture, the prophet Nephi was a Grade A faithful badass. He beheaded a drunk king, fled Jerusalem, hung in the wilderness with his deadbeat brothers until he built a ship, hit the seas, and landed in the Americas around 590 BC, where he ruled as the patriarch of the God-fearing folks kicking it in the West.

My dog of the same name shared none of the prophet's piety. So prolific were Nephi-the-dog's sexual encounters that word spread in our tiny California logging town, and, just for fun, a local pair of sketchy identical twins would lure strange dogs over to the Goolsby house knowing that Nephi would take on anything: Labradors, Dalmatians, Boxers, big dogs, small dogs; once, a massive orange cat.

When my mom suggested to my dad that we get Nephi fixed, if nothing else but to stop the sex show on our front lawn, my dad adamantly refused.

"Neutering makes them weird," he said.

—z—

When I call my dad and tell him I'm going in for a vasectomy he says, "Oh." It sounds like "Ooooooohhh." Just one word, that's all I get, but the tone, the extra time he gives the one syllable, sends me back to my childhood, watching Nephi pace back and forth on our driveway, the twins lurking somewhere. Later that evening, I pick up the vasectomy pamphlet the doctor gave me, and case the "Possible complications include" section for any behavior-related issues.

A week later, my dad and I talk again.

"Before you tell me about the kids," he says, "just tell me, this thing you're having done is voluntary, right?"

—z—

Nephi dies on a Saturday morning while I work my high-school summer job at an old-fashioned soda fountain. I'm wiping my shirt clean of a strawberry milkshake accident when my dad comes in and tells me that he's buried the dog out on a forested hill east of town. For a few moments I can't move, then I place my hands on the Formica counter, instantly conjuring the memory of the first time I stayed home alone for a few hours—how darkness came and frightened nine-year-old me and Nephi curled up by my side. My dad gives me a quick hug and leaves.

The following day I go to pay my respects, but I'm too late. Nephi has been dug up and largely devoured—we think—by a bear.

—

I'm a fifteen-year-old Boy Scout at summer camp, and the rumor is that the California Department of Fish and Game tranquilizes troublemaking black bears from Yosemite and transports them up for a second chance in my backyard (and summer camp location), Lassen Volcanic National Park. It's a calm July afternoon and I'm napping in my tent when the shouts of "bear" arrive. I jump out of the tent, my mind spinning images of gargantuan, blood-soaked beasts. I peer towards the spot where everyone points, across a yellow grass clearing, maybe fifty yards away. The bear is smaller than I feared, a gorgeous, glowing blonde with its nose in the air. I hear my inner voice say black bear, my mind already trying to reconcile the description. Our scout leaders blow into small whistles and one idiot kid steps forward and unsheathes his camera before being yanked back. The blonde bear starts slowly in our direction, and it's then that we're rounded up quickly and led away. As we trudge our way up a hill, the two camp counselors who had taught us black powder shooting and hatchet throwing earlier in the week come screaming by us, heavy rifles and black powder horns in hand, headed for our camp and the bear. They are dressed as frontiersmen: buckskin pants, thin, half-buttoned shirts, wide-brimmed hats. Earlier, during the hatchet lesson, they proudly claimed that they hadn't showered in two weeks, "like mountain men." As they pass I hear one of them say, "Goddamn."

A safe distance away, near the rudimentary showers and chow hall, our group is told to sit in a circle. Our fidgety Scout Master passes melting chocolate chip granola bars around and then folds his arms.

"Must be an asshole Yosemite bear," he says. "Our food was up in the trees." I'm not sure whom he's talking to because he stares down at the dirt between his feet. He puts his hand to his mouth.

"We'll hear the shot," the kid next to me says excitedly. "We're close enough."

No one says anything, all of us chewing as quietly as possible, waiting for the echo.

———

After the *Risky Business* episode, I decide I need an answer on the possible masturbation-makes-you-go-to-hell situation. The HBO free trial is running out and my desires aren't on any downslope that I can perceive. I work up the nerve and finally ask the bishop. He tries his best, and walks me through some lust tangents that seem to all center around the idea that sex is the most beautiful thing in the world, but only in the missionary position with a wife trying to bear children. The advice is to the effect of, "Have sex like Jesus is watching."

Even today, I'm not sure what that means, or, more terrifying, what that looks like. Christ at the footboard keeping score? Worse yet, suggesting improvements? When we get to it my trusted advisor tells me my masturbation question isn't addressed directly in scripture. That doesn't prevent him from saying, "Go check out the story of Onan and pray about it."

—⁓—

Onan's story in four sentences: (1) Onan, son of Judah, has a brother named Er who God kills because...well, it's not specified. (2) Judah (through God) tells Onan to sleep with Er's now widowed wife, so she can produce offspring. (3) Onan is rocking and rolling with said widowed wife, when he pulls out and "spills his seed on the ground," pissing off God. (4) God slays Onan.

Fourteen-year-old mind translates: So, don't pull out early if you're having sex with your dead brother's wife, or God will kill you.

—⁓—

It's 9 a.m., and I'm twenty-one years old. It's the morning after I've lost my virginity in a Colorado Springs hotel room to my college girlfriend. I walk through a parking lot, swinging my car keys in a small orbit around my index finger, now convinced that all the songs about making love until the sun comes up are full of shit. I take in the front range of the Rocky Mountains—sky-high Pike's Peak with its pockets of green pine, and to the south, some nasty, dark gray weather moving in fast. I consider the fact that I now live in a world where I've had sex; I'm a little surprised I feel good, but mostly the same. I try my hardest to focus on the joy, the fun awkwardness, the fact that I may get to do it again, and push away any thoughts of spiritual doom, but as I get to my car the weather arrives: a massive dust storm blanketing the sky in a dizzying mash of spinning brown. This is no regular storm; it crescendos into a reckoning of earth and sky, dry lightning pounding among vortexes of zooming grit.

I sit in my car and turn off the radio and wait. I hear the wind and dirt pounding at the windows; I feel the car oscillate, and although I believe myself 100% deity-free (for years at this point), my first thought as I slide the key in the ignition: *I picked the night before the apocalypse to piss off God.*

I'm twenty-eight years old and Sarah and I have been try-ing to start a family for six months with no luck. The sex is getting tense and our conversations about sex are getting tense so we decide to lie to the doctors. We tell them we've been trying for a year so we can get an appointment to see what's going on. One of the first things they have me do is provide a semen sample. I comply with the request in a specially furnished hospital room with clear plastic on the couch and drawers full of oddly titled pornography (*Nugget? Lemon People?*).

Soon, we learn that my sperm have "square heads," and that this could be an issue going forward. As we get the news I picture mini-hammerhead sharks swimming around in my testicles. I say, "Like mini-hammerhead sharks?" but the doc shakes his head and Sarah is crying into her palms so I shut up after that. It's here that I realize Sarah wants this more than I do, or at least is more serious about it. I want to be a dad, but I'm not sure why except that I think I'd be a good father. I visualize Little League games and bike rides, skinned knees and goodnight stories. But this optimistic collage is all I have, and I worry that it's not good enough.

I reach to rub Sarah's back and she lets me. The doc lets her cry for a bit before telling me to avoid saunas and hot tubs, and to eat more fruit and test again in six months.

Two months later Sarah finds out she's pregnant; we celebrate with Chinese food and water, but it's too soon. A few weeks after our Sweet and Sour Pork, on a cloudy Monday morning, she doubles over outside the gym. The abdominal pain twists her, forces her knees and hands to the sidewalk: an ectopic pregnancy.

Back from the hospital, Sarah rests her head on my lap as I run my fingers through her hair.

"We have to wait three months," she says. "Three months from today, we'll try."

—

Ella, our eldest daughter, was born on a Monday.

—

I'm two years old. My brother Jacob is born on a Monday.

My mom has her tubes tied immediately after the delivery. She'll tell me later that she decided it was time because she had all the children she could ever need: two healthy boys.

One day, a few months after Jacob's birth, my parents grow worried after he refuses to feed. My mom repeatedly coaxes his mouth to her nipples, but nothing. By evening, his tiny body turns a shade of purple. My parents drop me off with my grandparents and drive the three hours south to a special children's hospital in Sacramento. A week later, Jacob's heart and breathing stop there.

Amidst the emotional devastation is the fact that my parents have little money. Funeral and transportation arrangements will be difficult.

The morning after his passing, a nurse my parents have grown close to comes into the private waiting room and shuts the door.

"You do what you want," she says, "but I know you live a couple hours away. It'll be hundreds of dollars to transport Jacob to the mortuary. I want you to know that there are options."

"Can we take him?" my dad asks. "Can we take him to the mortuary?"

"You can do what you want. He's your child."

After some legal paperwork the nurse hands Jacob, wrapped in a white towel, to my parents. The nurse has taped the seams so it won't open in the car. She leads my parents to the back freight elevator and presses the ground floor button. My parents ride the elevator down alone and walk my brother across the parking lot. It has just rained and the car's door handle is wet. My dad places Jacob in the backseat of their car, but my mom tells my dad to put him in the child seat, so he does, trying to locate Jacob's back in the bundle to position him correctly. Dad stretches the safety harness across and snaps it together. When my dad starts up the car the radio comes on loud, and my parents both shoot their arms out to turn the volume down.

—z—

I don't remember Jacob. Calling him my brother sounds right and honest and healthy, but here's what I have: (1) two photographs: one of his months-old body spidered with clear hospital tubes trying to keep him alive, another with the whole family at Christmas; (2) rumors of a tape recording of his funeral held by a cousin in Utah; (3) my father telling me one night, unprompted, that the nurse all those years ago smelled like baby powder, that it was raining when she wrapped Jacob up, that he thinks Boz Scaggs was on the radio when he and my mom reached to turn the volume down.

—∕—

I'm thirty-three years old, walking home from the bus stop, off a little earlier than normal from Pentagon duty. It's early autumn and the first Halloween decorations have just begun to appear in doorways and front lawns. As I near my home I see Sarah and our three kids from across the street. They have yet to see me, and I pause for a moment and watch the four of them—Sarah on the front doorsteps cradling our newborn, Abby, and Ella and Owen scribbling with sidewalk chalk, not yet slugging one another. It's in this completely routine moment that I realize I'm a father. Why this fact hasn't felt as incredibly powerful to me before, I'm not sure—there have been thousands of similar scenes, more telling moments of responsibility, minor hardships, and moments of extreme pride—but this Wednesday afternoon the epiphany overtakes me, and I drop my computer bag and sob on the street corner.

The next day three-year-old Owen bounds from the sidewalk and chases his bouncing ball into the street, right in the path of a speeding minivan. The sound of screeching tires and my scream freezes Owen in the middle of the road. I know I'm watching his death, and the van's slow-motion stop gives me time to see Owen's wide eyes on me, his arms at his side, his blue "I'm the Big Brother" T-shirt, an elm tree in the median, the heavy, red van closing and closing in and closing in, but somehow stopping just in time, the front bumper gently nudging my son's shoulder.

—∕—

Still fresh from the vasectomy doctor's he'd-faint-and-the-bear-will-eat-him zinger, I haul Ella and Owen to the zoo. As we stroll the grounds I find myself sizing up the various animals, trying to determine which ones I could take down one on one. It's stupid, but my vascular prowess has been questioned and I need a theoretical win. From the animals we see that day, the no-way-in-hell list includes (but is not limited to): lion, elephant, rhinoceros, hippopotamus, tiger, gorilla, moose, anaconda, oryx, and cheetah. I give myself a fighting chance against a beaver, a smaller ostrich, prairie dogs, and most salamanders. I let it slip to the kids that I think I could take an otter one-on-one and Ella asks, "How about a giraffe?" I want to say yes, but among the other issues (stomping feet, massive frame, neck swings), I wouldn't know where to start: bite the leg? Still, I say, "Probably."

Finally, I mention seeing bears to the kids, but they show little interest. I offer cotton candy and soon we're standing in front of a pair of slobbering grizzlies. They're impressive enough, but what really catches my eye is another exhibit off to the side that no one's paying attention to: speckled bears.

If a large sloth and raccoon mated, it would look something like a speckled bear, with its small frame and beige mask-like markings across its face. Reading the small plaque, I learn that their natural habitat is exclusive to the Andes Mountains of South America. They're non-confrontational, solitary animals that just want to eat some plants and be left alone. The two in the enclosure may go two hundred pounds each, if that. They're lounging in a thin rectangle of shade, and I search for sizable teeth or claws, but there's nothing of note. I don't tell the kids and they don't ask, but I mentally add the speckled bear to the fighting chance list.

—✎—

A week and a half after my vasectomy I decide to stay up late and masturbate for the first time post-op. Around midnight, with Sarah and the kids fast asleep, I head downstairs, grab a couple tissues, and sit in the dark. I'm terrified. I pull down my shorts and place my hands on my legs. The two days of frozen peas on my groin, slow decrease of meds, and pain-free days of taking it easy have given me a shallow confidence that this will go well, but now, sitting in the night, I feel my heart working inside me as I consider my rerouted testicles. I close my eyes and begin to sift through my go-to visions: Sharon Stone in *Basic Instinct*, Angelina Jolie in the unrated *Original Sin*, some blonde beauty in a porn about pirates, but nothing works. I will my hand to my penis, but I can't move. I'm melting with nervous energy, listening for creaks on the stairs, and searching for any way out of this. It's then that I send out a wish for a way to come without touching myself, some on-demand, waking wet dream. I open my eyes, but there's only darkness and heartbeat.

I attempt a silent pep talk: *Everything is okay! You can do this! You are a man! You'll soon be able to make love to Sarah consequence-free! It will be fun! You can do this! Basic Instinct! Basic Instinct!* but I hear the intern's "Oops," and I keep seeing his back to me as we leave the room. I run my hands down my thighs and breathe. Then, a miracle: my mind flashes me an image of a topless female pirate. I summon enough courage to grab my penis, but I don't yet move my hand. *If something happens*, I think, *then it happens.*

—〰—

A little over a month later I wear my Air Force uniform and ride the DC metro into the Pentagon with my laptop, a book on the history of airpower, my notebook, a few pens, and a small plastic container of my semen. I've accomplished my twenty masturbation sessions, and it's time to see if the operation has taken.

At the clinic I hand the container to a smiling man behind the counter.

"Sample provided within the last two hours?" he asks loudly.

"Yep," I whisper and glance over my shoulder.

He studies the cup then wiggles it.

"It's like the opposite of a pregnancy test," I say. "You know, hoping for nothing."

He nods.

"Someone will call you soon," he says.

Nine hours later my doc calls me and starts out, "Everything's just fine, but we can't clear you yet."

The doc is still talking, but the voice goes white noise for a few seconds as I imagine reentering the minor surgery operating room, a new intern, the cauterizing machine warming up.

"You still have a few swimmers."

I hold the phone to my ear and feel the sweat squeezing through my forehead pores. I come to and there's a chuckle over the phone line.

—〰—

Just to be sure, I give it fifteen times then head back to the clinic. No jokes as I hand the sample over. Nine hours later, "All clear. You're good to go."

—

One of the identical twins that used to lure prospects to Nephi now works for the Forest Service. On a recent trip home I run into him on Main Street. He's a shouter.

"Remember Nephi?" I ask.

"Dude was crazy! Cra-zy! I mean, anything, man!"

I tell him about my operation, the doc's bear quote, Boy Scout camp.

"First of all, screw Yosemite!" he says. "They're still sending us their crap. Second, you're wrong. Bears will eat you, man! Why wouldn't they? It doesn't matter. Black bear, Griz, little bear, big bear, whatever. If it's hungry it's going to feed! I've seen 'em eat metal! They're sure as shit eating a person. That doc was right, man. She was right!"

A pause.

"Oh," I say, but it sounds like, "Ooooooohhh."

—

For the record, I've only fainted once: after giving blood. I had just stood up when the world went dark. I woke up to someone tapping my cheek, saying, "Breathe. Breathe."

They gave me low-grade orange juice and sent me on my way.

Since then, I never look when they stick the needle in.

—

Every now and then, Sarah will be out somewhere with our three kids and I find myself home alone. I revel in the arresting silence—a few minutes of precious peace. But when they're late getting home with no call, no text, my mind allows about an hour cushion, and then begins the murmurs of worst-case what-ifs. The whole scene flashes by: the dreaded call—auto accident, mass funeral, depression, insurance money, survival guilt, changing everything, moving (would I have to move? yes, definitely), different career, different clothes, new music, keep the photos, and later, me dating or not, the guilt accompanying either option, a second try at a family, reverse vasectomy?—and I can't help but take note of everything around me.

I track the physical details of the moment, possibly the last where my world remains intact, the smells, the weather, and it's all too much and I feel lightheaded, but then the garage door grumbles open and they all saunter in screaming at one another. Sarah simply forgot to turn her phone on again.

~

I'm thirty-four years old and a close friend comes over to the house. He's prone to exaggeration. After a few Yuenglings, he skips the question most have asked (why a vasectomy?) and asks me why Sarah and I decided to have children in the first place. Still debating starting a family himself, he wants an answer outside the majority of predictable replies: joy of teaching and nurturing and learning, ready to give and receive love, societal/familial/personal expectations. Nothing comes to me. The list he mentions pretty much covers the bases. I tell him so, and he seems disappointed.

"Not enough reasons?" I ask.

"So much can go wrong," he says. "Yes, a lot can go right, but it's easier for it to go wrong. You got diseases, drunk drivers, molesters, tornadoes, Republicans, drowning, drugs. And what if they just turn into jerks?"

What he wants to ask, but doesn't, is—Is it worth it?

Late that night I show my buddy out and circle back to the refrigerator. On the freezer door, Ella's crayon drawing of our family shows me as a stick figure tall in the center, with blue hair, blue eyes, blue arms, blue crotch, blue legs, and a green "Daddy" haloing above. It's a moment ripe for epiphany. If it were a movie scene, this is when the soft piano would bleed in as I wipe the gathering tears from my eyes. But there's nothing new this night, no realization or enlightenment, perhaps just some pride at how tall I'm rendered and that I'm smiling, and that's enough. I just want someone to remember me.

I hear the hum of the heater and note the microwave clock's 1:24, so I walk to each of my kids' rooms and bedside pause for a few seconds. I look at them and listen. I make sure they're all wrapped up tight and safe and breathing.

Sovereignty

I sit down at a Mexican restaurant in Hawthorne, Nevada, with Sarah, the woman that will become my wife, when, a few booths over, a young Spanish-speaking couple begin to argue, so I pull the whole *ignore, but really look* routine, but during my quick glance I see their infant daughter—browning, fading toward maroon, oddly silent, no, choking—and the parents have no clue, it's all lightning quick Spanish, a tap to the baby girl's cheeks, hands waving, and the whole place goes mute and I feel an invading, communal pause of fear and guilt—and then I'm there, at their table, all at once, body on fire, snatching the baby, flipping her face down in my hands when I see my palm strike her lower back, once, twice, again, again, but still no sound, and I roll her back over and her skin so dark and her mouth open and her glassed eyes and I look around the dimly lit restaurant that's giving up on me, and everything slows, and I should know what to do, I was an Eagle Scout years ago, but we practiced on adults, and I glance around this place and everyone sits in an eager forward lean, except for

the cook, ignoring the smoke behind him, and I know I'm
going to watch this baby die and I raise my hand to pound
the child again when the father yanks her from me, slams
her on the table and jams his finger into her mouth, he
pokes and digs, there's no way this is right, I will see this
child die, and he thrusts straight into her mouth, stuffing
his index finger to the knuckle, and I want to seize the
baby back and I shout *No! No!* and I touch his shoulder
and grasp the baby's limp arm and the father pushes me
in the chest and the mother jumps at me and pushes me
and unloads a string of Spanish curses, so I back up into a
dizzying space near the cash register, and the father pokes
and pokes, and then it's birthed—a garbled cry, a gasping
cry, a full-throttle cry, tiny limbs jolt back into motion and
he lifts his resurrected baby to his chest and he sits on the
dirty restaurant carpet and sobs.

Two years later, I drive home from work in Cambridge,
England, and I come across a group of people surround-
ing a boy and his damaged bicycle in the middle of a side
street and I jump out of my car in my Air Force uniform
and for some reason everybody makes way and I walk right
up to scan then touch the boy and someone says *He was
hit* and I ask the boy if he can feel his body and he says
Murky and I tell him not to move, but he says he's fine
and I point and yell at a woman to call emergency services
and someone asks if I'm American and I say *Yes* and they
respond *Where did you come from?* and I say *I live around
the corner* and they ask where my base is, but this boy is in
shock, *Please*, I say, and I see the fear in his eyes and I ask
him if he plays soccer, but I should've said football, and he
frowns and squirms under my touch and I hear the siren in
the distance and I say *Easy, Easy*, but he wiggles away from

me, lifts himself and the banged bike up, and pedals off, and before he rounds the corner an onlooking man asks if I'm bombing Iraq—I am—but I don't answer, I'm watching the boy bike away, I'm listening to the closing siren, and someone else asks *You live here? In this city?* Someone else says *At least you tried.*

It's 2008, outside the wolf cages at the Knoxville Zoo, and Sarah and I pass a small snack shop selling cotton candy and Cokes and fry bread, and a fat woman falls to the concrete and seizures, and the humid afternoon slants and everyone stands and stares and someone yells *Grab her tongue!* which I know is wrong, but I keep my mouth shut and squeeze Sarah's hand and lead her to the gorillas, where we watch the content males grunt and eat and play with themselves.

What My Dead Wife
Should Know

If you ever show yourself come alone and wear your black
hair down like the night we met in Provo, just don't look
at me like I've done something wrong.

If you're going to watch us please stay quiet, I'll always
be in recovery, and Janet lets little things distract her in
bed. Yes, I tell her I love her, and if you can read minds you
know that I try to convince myself these are the best days
of my life, even the fifth anniversary of your death, when
our only son left for Iraq.

I don't know what you thought watching Janet and me
in the shower as Dylan undressed near Kirkuk. Believe me,
I replay the scene: my fingertips on her body as thousands
of miles away electricity bolted through Dylan's soapy
feet, ricocheted among his organs until he collapsed in the
soiled shower.

Do you know that I believed them when they said he
grabbed a live wire? The Army officers sat in pressed green
uniforms where we used to stage the lit Christmas tree,
and I nodded along like an ignorant child. I even conjured

it as truth: Dylan on his wet tiptoes reaching at the electrical wires above. They told me it wasn't shoddy contractor work, it wasn't a mortar or a suicide bomber, it was our child, showering and reaching up to grab a live wire. They told me he wasn't the only one.

If you can come to me, then you were there, by the yellowed birch trees and polished casket, our son just one of fourteen accidents sinking into the earth without wartime medals, and I, hearing Janet's veiled sobs, I needed you there.

If you ever catch me alone speak to me. Maybe you can back it all up to the moment Dylan returned from the dusty patrol. Whisper his slow motion-disrobe as he peels away his rifle, helmet, vest, body armor, boots, blouse, pants, socks, shirt, underwear. His body was our bodies.

Everyone knew what to call me when you died, but no one says widower to your face. Now, there's no name for what I am, but sometimes I try to think of one. It's always at dawn, when I rise alone and find myself in the basement, opening up old photos of holidays, but I can't give the feeling language.

I promise, I won't ask about God, but remember, come alone, 'cause I won't hold up if Dylan's here, floating around like the helium-filled balloons we used to give him as a kid. I remember. He'd rub up the static and hold the balloon above the top of his head so his hair would stand. Then he'd ground it on the carpet and sit on the balloon. We'd watch him together. We knew what was coming, but we wanted him to learn. We'd watch him together, awaiting the inevitable pop.

Benevolence

One night I'm watching television alone, my mind breaking from class prep on Raymond Carver's short stories,
and up pops a show about people helping one another, real
heroes, fresh food to orphanages in Thailand, people dropping their lives, unloading money to strangers on back-
streets, healthy college kids massaging the elderly in Des
Moines, circumcision and home building in Guatemala,
children and adults sobbing and suffering, then healing
embraces and peace, all under stringy music that squeezes
couch loafers' tear ducts tight, and behind my dry, stable
eyes I think: I'm a prick.

So, I'm in a mood, and not just because of the show—
my confession is that I pretty much deserve the label: I
never return my sister's calls. I've stolen from neighbors
(tools) and stores (CDs and produce). I haven't forgiven
my father for believing in God, and even refused to at-
tend my mother's funeral because of my father's insistence
on prayer and hymn. I've never set foot in a soup kitchen

or raised money for breast cancer. I'm ruthless with other people's faults, and I gossip. I tell millions of insignificant lies that help me, and believe me, it doesn't bother my sleep.

This may not sound like much, and it's true, I've never killed anyone, but the damn show and its Thai orphans have me contemplative. I know I can't turn everything around, and, frankly, I don't know if I want to, but the one thing that pisses me off is that I'm alone, a thirty-year-old graduate school student with books and ideas and few friends.

I resolve to do something the next day. After all, benevolence has its benefits, but when I wake up I'm thinking about my class of college freshmen, about how I'm going to sell a story about a blind man, a jealous husband, and a homosocial living room drawing to eighteen-year-olds at a state school, and it isn't until lunch, when I overhear Abe, the fat, Shakespeare expert, mention the same sentimental television show I'd viewed the night before in the break room. Abe's in his fifties, his belly-chest mound testing his suspenders' elasticity. Whenever I run into him my inner voice says heart attack, and I imagine fumbling with AED patches and shocking the wrong side of his chest.

Abe maneuvers near Elliot, a red-haired poet from Lubbock, who at last year's drunken end-of-year party mentioned a threesome in college. A week after the party, I went to one of her readings. She wore loose clothes that hid her vegetarian figure, but there were still more men than women in the small auditorium. One of her poems elaborated on the different varieties of tomatoes, how they represented types of love and lust. Near the end, in her Texas twang, she rhymed "fucked" with "plucked" without breaking a smile, and I fell in love-lust on the spot. That night I told her the truth, that I loved her hair pulled back

off her face, and I lied and told her tomatoes were my fa-
vorites. Somehow, in my male mind, I thought this might
lead to sex, maybe even with her and a friend, but she told
me she hated tomatoes.

"But, your poem," I said.

"I'm a poet, Ethan."

Now, back in the lunchroom, Abe leans in tight to
Elliot as she rubs across a mushroom with a dull butter
knife.

"I didn't see the show, Abe," Elliot says, in reference to
the same television show that failed to move me.

"And the circumcisions," Abe says. "Of all the things
they can be doing down there in Guatemala, they choose
foreskin?" Abe scissors his right hand index/middle finger
combo.

I give the awkwardness just enough time to sink in, and
ask Abe, "Did you cry at the end?"

"Who doesn't cry?" he says. "All that music and those
old people in Iowa walking for the first time in years. In
Shakespeare's time…" And there it is: the transition to the
one thing in the universe he can speak to: good 'ol Shakespeare. I know the drill and quickly tune him out. I peer
around him, not an easy thing to do, and stare at Elliot
in side view, and watch the slippery mushrooms and dull
knife battle it out.

Later, when I walk by the lunchroom, Abe eats alone.
He consumes the same thing every lunch: lasagna and
grapes. The rumor is he buys a family-size lasagna each
Sunday, bakes it up, and chews through it Monday through
Saturday, then buys another. No one knows how often he
buys grapes, but they're always the purple ones.

It's one of the worst things to witness: a person alone
with his or her food, chewing and staring at the opposite

wall. Abe looks big in the tiny, white room. His shoulders are as wide as the table, and he rolls his sleeves and places his plastic knife and fork down after every bite. It's not like people can't stand Abe, but he lacks most of the normal social graces, and in conversation, no matter the subject, he steers to Shakespeare. Most days he eats alone. Most days he walks to his car alone. He tries to talk to people, but he's just annoying enough that most people fake a heavy workload and scramble. Rumor is, he used to be married, but I don't know if I believe it. I don't actually know a single thing about him besides his academic expertise, his dietary routine, and the fact that he's scared of water (another end-of-year party confession). Still, I walk on, leaving Abe with his lasagna.

When I return to my office, I pick up Carver and jump into a story about a fishpond, fathers, and grudges, and then I see Elliot pass in the hallway and hear my internal voice say, "My tomato." It's ridiculous, but I can't silence the voice, so I put the book down and try to clear my mind, but nothing works until I come to the mental image of Abe, all alone, slumped over, face down in his lasagna in the break room waiting for me to revive him. This new, pitiful image haunts me for a good minute before forcing me up into the hallway, break room bound. Steps away from the room, lightning strikes: I'm not that bad a guy. I'm acting right now out of kind, wholehearted, irrational concern. Then, a revelation: Abe can be my fresh fruit in Thailand, my backrub in Des Moines, my Guatemalan foreskin! And if Elliot notices my generosity, that wouldn't hurt my feelings one bit. Hell, word would spread around the department quickly, and that can only help. So, I step into the lunchroom as fat Abe chews his last two purple grapes and pull up a seat, and even though I think I know the answer, I ask him if he's ever fished before.

It's slow going at first. We start with bobbers and worms from lawn chairs on the rocky shore. Well, I should say, we're near the shore. In the beginning, Abe insists on staying back thirty feet from the shoreline—he says he's not scared of the water, he just needs distance from it—so I cast for him and let the line out as I walk back to him and hand him the pole.

Abe is surprisingly eager, though you'd never know it by his demeanor. He never smiles on our outings, but he sits and holds his pole, and asks me about the strength of the line (10 lb test), what he should do if he hooks into one (just reel like hell), if we let it go or keep it (we're keeping his first). Basically, I'm playing dad, and to be honest, I enjoy having someone with me. At a minimum, it balances out all the other ways I'm a below average human.

And people have noticed. Colleagues joke with me at first, but after a couple outings with Abe, I see their jealous faces in the hallways as if they missed the opportunity to be the "good" guy or girl. Even my department head, who I've talked to maybe five times in my life, stops by one day and tells me he thinks I'm doing a great job, and I consider asking him what part of my studies or teaching he's referring to, but I keep my mouth shut, and as he leaves, he gives me a thumbs up and says, "Thank you."

Every fishing morning, Abe shows ten minutes early in his 1991 tan Toyota Camry. I can't get him to stop playing Heart, and after a few trips I actually look forward to "Crazy on You."

Seven fishing trips in, and I know a lot more about Abe: he grew up in Syracuse until he was ten, before his family moved to Yuma to escape the cold. He sings in a community chorus (tenor). He thinks the department head is a dick, and he knows 99 percent of his students are morons. His fear of water? He nearly drowned in a neighbor's pool when he was twelve. I find out his wife left him on a cloudy afternoon after telling him about a man she met online. Abe shares this one evening driving back to my apartment, Croce softly in the background.

"So, she has her suitcase and plane tickets," Abe says. "I'm sitting in the living room eating a sandwich, and of course I start crying. My chest feels like it's ripping apart. And we go back and forth. She says, 'I don't owe you an explanation,' like that settles it. I can't think of anything to say. Things weren't great, but they weren't bad. The same as everyone. So, I can't think of anything to say, but I blurt out 'What's his name?' and she says 'Vegas84.' 'What the hell is Vegas84?' I say, but you already know. It's his web ID or whatever. Doesn't even give me the guy's name. 'That's all you need to know,' she says. So, that's all I know."

"Jesus," I say.

"Yep," he says.

"How'd yours get away?"

"I'm sorry?"

"Your ex."

And when I let him know I've never been married, his face slumps into disappointment. Perhaps he hoped my story wouldn't be too different from his. So, I tell him about my father, how he believes that all the actions of his and everyone else's life are the result of a caring God, that there's a plan for everyone, even my youngest sister who was hit by a car when she was eight. I tell him how Carrie's physical trainer comes over three times a week to bend her legs for her. It's been twenty years, and she endures the agonizing therapy hoping to walk one day, but it's never going to happen, and yet my dad says stuff like, "If it's God's will." I laugh a sarcastic laugh.

Abe says, "Your dad's right."

I turn my head and stare at Abe driving his old Toyota. I wait for a "just kidding," or, "I'm screwing with you," but Abe doesn't cuss, and his hands stay at ten and two, and his vision remains straight on the road. I'm so angry I could hit him, but I play the quiet routine all the way home, and when I get out and collect my gear, I'm about to say something about his weight or his fat ex-wife or Vegas84, but he beats me to it, says, "Ethan. You should believe in God."

After two weeks of avoiding Abe, he swings by my office.

"Saturday?" he asks, and I almost regret having told two colleagues Abe's wife-leaving story.

"We're sitting right up on the water," I say pointedly.

That Saturday Abe and I sit on the shoreline in our flimsy chairs when his pole flutters ever so slightly. He wears a red lifejacket, and the tip of his pole barely bends, but Abe pops up and thrusts the pole into my chest.

"Reel the bastard in, Abe," I say, putting my hands in the air like I'm innocent.

And so he does. Abe reels like a mad man, leaning back, belly out, and the pole still barely bends—I'm thinking it's a stick—so I say, "Might be a stick," but Abe's not listening; he burns the line in, and this is fishing's eden: the quick jolt, the invisible fight below the surface, the pressure and power. You never know if you're going to have a battler on your hands, so I keep on him, "Go. Go. Go. Do it, Abe,"

I say, and he does; he lets out a "Woo," and he reels all the way to the end when the bobber crests, and he rears back one final time and yanks the pole, and a tiny bluegill flies out of the water and lands near our feet. Somehow he's hooked the thing through the gills. I lean down to pick the fish up, but I'm so excited for Abe, I stand and offer a high five, but he refuses. And it's then, with my hand still in the air, that I notice his flushed face, his hands already on the top of his head pulling at his thinning hair.

"Throw it back. Throw it back. Throw it back," he says quickly and softly.

"It's your first, Abe," I say.

"Back," he says.

I hold the fish in my hands, and it squirms because the damn hook is in good.

After a few seconds I know I'm going to have to cut the line. Abe leans in.

"Are you getting it out?" he says.

"Abe. You don't have to look."

"Is it stuck?"

I turn my back to Abe and in one motion snip the line and wheel and fling the bluegill back into the lake.

After the "throw it back" incident, I guess we're done with fishing altogether, but the next Wednesday, Abe shows up at my office holding waders that look twenty years old. It makes no sense. It took us seven trips just to get up to the shoreline.

"You think you might be rushing it?" I say.

"I got these at a yard sale. They're waders," he says. "You can go in the water, but not get wet."

"That's true."

"I'm ready," he says.

"We'll take it easy."

"Did you know there's fishing in Shakespeare?" he says.

One night I'm loading up my shopping cart with Ramen noodles. It's about all I can afford from my measly teaching stipend, and for some reason I haven't tired of them. I throw the fourth huge bundle on top when Elliot taps me on the shoulder. Chicken and beef flavored noodles fill my entire cart. She asks me how I am, and without any logical explanation I hear myself say, "Just buying Ramen for the homeless."

Elliot likes this enough to have dinner with me later that night. I hide the Ramen in my closet. Elliot wears a red sundress and brings wine. She's pulled her hair back, and I can see the small freckles that dot her cheeks. During dinner—trout I'd caught on the river and four ears of corn I stole from a farmer's market—she doesn't lean toward me. She's polite and laughs at my nervous jokes, but I can't help but notice that she looks at me like she doesn't expect anything different from me than the thousands of other men she's met in her life. After the meal we sit out on the cramped balcony and watch the yellow city lights. There's a Little League game a block away, and I hear the young announcer calling out pitch counts. Nothing's wrong, but neither Elliot nor I say anything for awhile. A car in the parking lot starts up.

"I played baseball," Elliot says. "And not softball. Little League against the boys."

"I played against a girl," I say. "She was good." That's a lie.

"They hated it when I got a hit," she says. "I remember pitchers crying if I hit off of them. And of course, all the fans would clap and whisper, 'she's a girl,' 'did you see that?,' 'a girl hit a double.' The other team's fans would clap for me. Pathetic."

"One team in my league had two girls," I say, then realize I should just shut up and let her talk.

"I hit a homer once, and I forgot to touch second," Elliot says. "Instead of calling me out, they wanted me to go and run the bases again. Free pass."

"There's a poem."

"But I didn't," she says, and pauses. "I stayed in the dugout." When she proudly says the last bit, her tone changes—a touch higher—and I figure she's pushing the facts.

I think to myself, just let her talk, but I say, "Hard to believe you just stayed there."

I watch Elliot inhale. There's traffic nearby and the muffled applause of the game. I hear my apartment-mate come in two hours early. He yells, "Smells like fish." I excuse myself and run in to let him know the situation. When I return, Elliot's chair is half a foot closer to mine. The ball field lights click off one by one.

"Sorry," I say. "He doesn't like fish."

She doesn't look at me when I sit.

"I didn't stay in the dugout," Elliot says. "I jogged the bases. Slowly. And I don't care what you say. I liked it." A pause. "And yes, it would make a great poem."

She smiles and touches my arm, and suddenly I'm alive and strong, and I consider if I should say it, then I do: "The Ramen noodles are mine. They're stashed in my closet."

One time Abe takes me to breakfast before heading out to the river, and I watch him pound three servings of pancakes, butter, no syrup.

"I thought you only ate Lasagna and grapes."

"I thought you only ate that noodle shit."

After eating, we drive out to the river, and the mosquitoes swarm us as Abe and I practice casting on the riverbank.

At one point I have to take Abe's hands in mine and fling the line out together so he understands what a good cast feels like. And then we're in the water, and Abe, in his past-prime waders, says, "Can't feel the water. Not in it." The dark water rises up to our hips as we cast at a fork of a muddy tributary creeping into the main river. The afternoon is clear, and I pull in four fish before Abe gets a hang of it and starts casting where he aims.

It's not perfect, but Abe's happy and we talk about our English department, and then about fishing, and I even let Abe lecture me about the weakness of Othello and the glory of Twelfth Night, and he tells me that Shakespeare was the last writer to pen happy endings, but I don't feel like arguing.

Then the rhythm of the casting takes over like a day-time lullaby and I absorb the muddy bottom of the river and the cottonwoods and the warm sun. I feel myself slip into a comfortable rhythm as I cast toward a shadowed spot near a boulder, time and again. I see the lure splash onto the shadow, and I think about how my father taught me to fish years ago, and then about Elliot, how I like her lies—apparently, there was no threesome in college—how I like her poems that have nothing to do with her. Then my line snags and I come to and hear myself say "shit." I'm tugging and tugging and popping my rod because I really don't want to disturb the shadows, and I hear Abe's voice, a distorted "Ethan," and again, "Ethan," strained and nervous. When I turn around, he's somehow far from me and slightly sunk under the surface of the water where the main river current meets our sluggish tributary. I see the afternoon river pour into his waders, taking him under. I try to move, but the water and the mud slow me and I yell to Abe, "Cut it. Cut your shoulder straps." I cut the air with my index/middle finger combo and then mime cutting my straps. The cold current wraps and weighs his body, and I know he doesn't have a knife for his old waders. Suddenly, I'm out of my waders and swimming at Abe's distant neck and face and raised hands bobbing and moving away from me, and then he's under, just his thrashing arms show, then his white face bobs up, gasping. I'm thrashing and getting nowhere as he floats downstream, further from me. I see Abe's arms, then his face burst up from the river with his open mouth and closed eyes, now carried by the full force of the main river's current. He goes under again with his hands just above the surface, and I see his hands for awhile, just his white palms, and once more his forearms thrashing, and his elbows, then just his hands. Then one hand on the surface. Then nothing, but water, and more water. I wait with my blasting heart for his hand, his head, or his back, but there's nothing except insects and summer and a gentle breeze. The river seems so calm and unburdened as it flows heavy downriver. I watch a tangle of brush and stags as I veer to the bank and stand in water to my hips and tremble in the shadows of bank trees. There should be noise, but it's quiet. Suddenly, a group of teenagers appear on inner tubes hugging the distant bank, far away, slowly floating in brightly colored shorts and bikinis under the clear sky. They don't feel my terror, and I watch them start around the bend just past the brush and stags. I want to shout to them, but something stops me. The world starts to spin, but I can still see the teenagers. I watch them, then hear the girl second from the back scream and raise her legs in the air and point at something in the water. Her scream makes me reach for my ears.

"So, Carver was a drunk, moved around all the time, was unhappy most of his life, and wrote stories about sad people and their miserable lives," says a dark-haired student in the third row. It's my third week back after Abe's death. She continues: "And the point of this story is that these two young people dancing in the guy's driveway are happy now, but they're going to be miserable just like this poor, melancholy guy with all of his possessions outside, when they should be inside?" But, it doesn't sound like a question.

That day, I eat alone. The significance is not lost on me. I see colleagues walk by, and when they notice it's me, their bodies lurch into a half stop. They want to say something, but they don't know what. They don't want me to eat alone, but they don't care enough to sit. Most stop and grab the doorjamb and wish me the best, or simply nod.

I realize I was wrong: eating alone isn't the worst. Sometimes it's nice to have distance and patience with food. I've gone through the odd pain and confused responsibility of the accident, and lately, I've wanted to be alone, but today Elliot walks in and sits with me. This is the worst: I know she's started to see someone from her gym, but she hasn't told me yet, and she sits across the table, and my god, she wears her hair back so I see all of her face. She puts her hands on the table, and I pray that she reaches across for my hands, but she doesn't. She tells me it's okay, that everything will be okay, but I don't think she believes it.

A couple months later, I find a seat in the back of the room as Elliot sips water on the undersized stage. The small auditorium is almost full when she launches into her first line of verse. Again, it's from memory: just Elliot in a blue dress, and she moves so fluidly in her slight space, her hips gently swaying, her sweeping gaze, and occasionally she closes her eyes and enters that place of self-listening and peace. But, something is off. The slant rhymes and pacing twist unconvincingly, and her introductions to the poems offer little insight. It's not overt, but the crowd knows what I know, and there's a collective murmur in between poems.

Elliot sips her water, and looks over the audience knowingly, and says, "This is new." All the rhymes vanish. Her pacing is quick then slow in the exact right spots, and the poem takes us to a boy-dominated ball field in Lubbock, Texas, where she grew up. The audience is there with her and the easterly wind that carried the 0-2 delivery she belted over the left field fence. We listen to her miss second base and sit in the dugout while the umpires and both coaches beg her to come back out and run the bases again. But she refuses to go until she spots her smoking, weathered father lean on the outfield fence. Something cracks inside of her in the dugout and she rises and runs the bases slowly, and we feel the way her twelve-year-old self soaks in her gender and the second, less enthusiastic applause. I hear the dusty squish of each base under her right-cleated foot and her raspy-voiced father cheering her name above it all for the first and only time. Then, after the game he comes to her and picks her up and says "Forget boys. You're my girl." She smells the Marlboros on her father's skin and feels the caked cement on his worked fingers as he brushes the infield dirt from her cheek. In the auditorium Elliot's voice cracks, then cracks again, and I feel my nose and eyes start up and Elliot wipes at her face. I want to run to her on the small stage, but I don't. She takes a sip of water and we're back with Elliot the girl, in her black-and-orange Giants Little League uniform as her father closes the door on his Chevy truck. He drives away as she waits for her mom to pick her up because that's who she lives with because the court says her parents can't be in the same place at the same time. She stands alone, waiting, and Elliot the poet pauses, then ends with her father's name—Gabriel— and I pull my wet hands away from my face.

I wait in line at the end to say hello. I want her to know that I came, for her to see my red eyes and say something. She notices me four people back from her and throws me a preemptive thank you smirk. And I think about her baseball poem. I want to believe it all, and I think about asking her if that's the real story as I move up in line. I remember our night on the balcony where I would have believed anything she told me as long as she didn't leave. Elliot folds her arms in front of her as she speaks to the one man between us. I overhear him talking about grape tomatoes. Then, unannounced, I think of Abe in the white lunchroom, on the rocky shore, stepping into the water for the first time. The images jumble together, and I replay the afternoon in the river, but this time he's close to me when the water pours into his waders, and instead of swimming to him as he's slowly swept downstream, I stand there and watch him wail and drown because I'm not a hero. I see myself entering the lunchroom the moment I decided to do something about Abe and his life, and asking Abe if he had ever fished before, and him thinking about it, chewing on his purple grapes, swallowing, and saying, "I'm not scared of water," or was it, "you should believe in God?" When I snap to the present, there's no one in front of me, just me and Elliot. She waits on my greeting, and I realize I no longer care if her poem is true. I just want Abe to eat alone. I want my sister to heal and walk again. I want to touch my dad's arm the morning we lower my mom into the ground. But, it's too hard to move to those places all at once, so I stand still, and after a moment, Elliot steps toward me, close enough for me to smell her lavender soap, close enough to take me some place where things end well.

Ishi Wilderness

Chief said there was this fire over in the Ishi Wilderness, and DeQuan was always on my ass about dropping some Molly as we fought fires across the north state, and not just weed again, but electric stuff that would morph me into the savior I was, and there was no smoke in the sky, no fires anywhere in the universe, so *Fine*, I said as we rolled in the back of the Cal-State Fire rig on Highway 36, and I stuck my tongue out like I used to do in church, and DeQuan placed the pill there and I kept it safe and warm for a bit just thinking about Kendra and if I'd ever lick her again, and Mister said, *We fight fires by lighting fires, isn't that weird to anyone?* but he was new and had his yellow contacts in so we told him to sit on his thick thumb and spin, *A thousand times*, DeQuan said, *I don't care if you were in the Marines, Mister, spin a million times*, and then the rig swung a left turn and we rammed into one another and *Swallow it*, he said, *You're a savior, You need to feel the world*, so I did, but Mister had his trencher in his hand saying, *I'll kill you Quan, I've killed kids, don't think I won't kill you*, and Mister let out a screech laugh, the same belly sound that Kendra laughed when I licked the back of her knees, low and full of hate, and I was there for a pulse with Kendra and her Mickey Mouse and tomahawk tattoos, but the road turned to dirt, to rocky dirt, and Mister had had enough and showed us his brown teeth, and someone said *Lightning, Matches, Campers, It doesn't matter,* and my legs were thinning out in my stiff pants, and my skin was alive and swaying when DeQuan asked, *Iraq or Afghanistan?* but Mister said, *Africa,* so I said, *Where's that?* and we parked by Mill Creek under Black Rock, and finally, smoke and rattlers everywhere, and Chief told us to watch the flames and watch our feet, and I was digging and digging the lines and sweating my lungs out while the flamethrowers started new fires, and I wondered if Kendra's girl was eight yet and then I wondered what would happen if these flames crested the hill and splashed all the way to Sacramento, and DeQuan took his gloves off and touched a lava rock and said, *It's warm, man, still warm,* and I said, *You know Mister was right, that dude will kill you,* but DeQuan didn't care about that because we were in the Ishi Wilderness fighting fire that lit the pines above us, yes, we dug like saviors, yes, like kings saving the promised land where Ishi watched his mother die, where he wandered out of the hills, the last of his people, and I wanted to touch the water and flames and the lava rock too, so I asked, *Is it still hot,* but DeQuan was dumping orange Gatorade over his face and shouting *Regeneration! Regeneration!* and Mister yelled, *A fucking arrowhead,* and held a pointed rock above his head, and I knew right then that Mister would die that day because of his sins, I could feel it on the tip of my hot nose, and later we found him in Mill Creek, face up, dead, but happy, because every dead person is happy in their own way, and later someone told me Mister was never in the Marines, had never killed any kids, although I understood why he'd lie about it because it's a lie that works, a special lie I used later at The Ranch House when a young drunk said my brother was a fag and I couldn't take another jail stint but wanted to see genuine fear, and another time the night before Kendra came in and said I was right to belt her kid, but I knew she was lying because she still wore the white hospital band, but I didn't care, no one wants to be alone, and she had dyed her hair red and drenched that jasmine perfume that curled my toes, so I bought her four Miller Lights and led her back to my place on Birch Street, and I tucked her girl in on the green sofa with my Oakland A's blanket and smelled her girl's dirty sweet smell when Kendra made her girl hug me goodnight, and then we went out on the back deck and watched the lit smoke of the lumber mill rise up into the night, and I took off Kendra's pants and turned my mini-Maglite on and spread her legs and touched her tattoos with my thumb, so soft and careful, first Mickey Mouse with a frown on her left thigh then a red and green tomahawk on the right, and I leaned in to lick them when she said, *Not tonight, Not tonight, Look,* and she held her left arm out to me and I saw the jagged scar on her inner forearm like she'd meant it, and when I went inside I heard her girl snoring and I knew Kendra wasn't worth it and her girl wasn't worth it, and I knew then that her girl would eventually crack her femur on the back of a Harley or catch a bad pill, so I let her sleep and snore because I had that incredible power, and I tried to sleep, but I heard Kendra rocking on the back deck probably fingering her scar and cursing the fact that it's so hard to die, so I gulped some NyQuil and listened to the deck creak under Kendra's chair, lulling me to sleep, her jasmine smell still in my nose, and I wondered if anyone else in the world was happier than me.

Not an Emergency

Standing in six inches of the summered Rouge River, outside Grants Pass, Oregon, I listen to my best friend, Tim, argue with his girlfriend about squirrels and the plague while a boy in red trunks gingerly enters the water next to us—"We shot every damn squirrel on our farm," Tim's girl says—and in my periphery, a silver flash catches my eye, and I swing around to see a flat-topped teenager in a black shirt level a shiny revolver at the still-dry chest of the nearby, red-suited boy.

Without prompt I feel my leap into the water, and I watch the green-brown murk swirl for what feels like a minute before I lift my eyes above the surface and take it in: the teenager still aiming the gun, curse-screaming, shaking the barrel left and right. And the targeted boy, near death, shins deep in the cold water, stares straight-faced calm into the firearm. It's all wrong, and I want to yell at the boy, to tell him to take this seriously; I want him as scared as I am of bullets in the afternoon; to respect fear, as I had learned to do as a boy his age, and yet he stands there under the summer sun, blinking into obscurity. The first shot sends me back below the water, and this time I keep my eyes closed and feel the river's current on my face, my throbbing neck, and through the porthole of my oxygen-deprived mind I relive my red-eyed father at the edge of my mother's deathbed, beckoning me to touch her. Convulsing for air as I crest the surface, I see the gunman and victim both standing, both whole. Somewhere, a bullet hurls its way toward the Pacific. I feel Tim's girl press up behind me as the soft white smoke from the gun dissolves into the sky. Suddenly, the gunman turns and dashes to his idling car—a brown Geo Metro, Idaho plates—and spins out, fires another shot into the air, and disappears. As the river-goers emerge from their feeble hiding places no one approaches the boy in the river, who opens his mouth and slowly touches his stomach and swimsuit-covered hips. We half surround him from afar and shake our heads, but no one goes near, no one asks if he's okay, no one questions what all of that was about, until someone says, "Will he come back?" and the boy says, "Yes." And then he sits in the shallows like a bathing child and cups the river water to his face.

I beg Tim to drive faster, and he does. We screech up to the first pay phone we see and I dial 9-1-1. I give it to the operator as fast as I can: revolver, shots, swimming hole, boy still there, brown Geo Metro, Idaho, 5'6", flattop, coming back, death, help, now, help. The operator thanks me, but there's something in her voice that isn't catching all of this, so I ask if the sheriff is on his way and she says no, they don't have enough people to respond to every emergency.

"The gunman will come back!"

"I'm sorry," the operator responds, "Yours is not an emergency."

I picture the boy sitting, playing in the water, alone at the deserted swimming hole, as the brown car pulls back up to finish the job.

———

"This is insane. You can't be serious," I say, and slam the receiver down after the reply.

On the winding drive back into town we're all silent. Tim keeps it under the speed limit, and the wind blows our hair through the open windows. I try to calm myself, and I look at the rocky hills and old, rundown houses that flash by. I realize that this is the first time I've dialed 9-1-1. I think of times when I didn't:

> when my mother's dialysis machine broke open halfway through a blood cycle, and I saw her dark blood on the tan carpet, so I ran to the kitchen and called the manufacturer of the machine because I was twelve and didn't know better.

> after I cut out holes in tennis balls and stuck them onto the feet of her walker so she could slide it on the kitchen floor, but she slipped and fell hard because I cut through worn, slick tennis balls, instead of newly opened neon felt.

> when my father asked me to rise from my hospital chair and come touch my dead mother "because it's just skin son, a shell" and I looked at my young hands and I couldn't get my legs to work and I knew I was going to need help doing anything from then on.

Outside Tim's neighborhood, he swerves the car to avoid a suicidal squirrel and his girlfriend brings up the plague again, how some idiots let the little devils eat from their hands, and she pantomimes getting bit after trying to feed a nasty plague carrier. Even after the act, her hands rattle in her lap. She reaches for the radio, but pulls back. Tim leans his head back on the driver's headrest and the car quiets again, as silent as the phone line after my mother's death, when I asked Tim to tell my teachers I wouldn't be in the next day.

As we round onto Tim's street, we pass a police car, lights off, patrolling the safe avenue, and I can't help but wonder what he's waiting for, what would get him to flick on the siren and fly to the rescue. A mother's eyes closing for the last time? A 17-year-old boy bowed in grief and loss? I wonder where he's driving as he heads east, away from the dusty swimming hole, and if he'll be the one that's forced to call in the divers to scrape the Rogue River for the boy we left alone.

Green Lungs, Purple Hearts, Orange Kidneys

George, you're a funny motherfucker. I see you there on TV at a midsummer press conference, straining those vowels out, dumb as shit, but sincere as shit, and I believe you, you want me to kill all these Samarra fuckers. You want me to come home clean and slide on up to the White House, smile nice and strong, and you'll pin that medal on my chest and we'll hug it out, Texas-style. You're a believer, a rich boy, but that's not your fault. You didn't want to be president, not really. You just wanted some pussy, but you blinked and you got America's pussy and damn it feels good. You got that Utah pussy and I was there, three weeks after graduation, in the recruiter's office, signing my name. I almost came on those enlistment papers they felt so good. I was there in Tarmiyah in 2005 with all of the shit and sand and the sniper that fucking picked us off. One of his bullets clipped my calf, and a few weeks later I stood at attention with my hobbled buddies and the Stars and Stripes, and they passed out Purple Hearts like a Christmas in hell. We were supposed to be serious during the ceremony, and for the most part we were, but do you know what we bullshitted about after? Slicked-back George Washington on the heart-shaped medals, that primped motherfucker in his wig looking serious and shit. Everyone knows we need a new portrait, and I said, "Let's put our George on there. Celebrate who sent us," but everyone started fucking around: "You want a mouth-breather like Bush on the medal?" Now don't get pissed, I defended you then, but it's 2007 and I'm back in the desert and I see you there on TV straining those vowels out, dumb as shit. It's 2007 and no one remembers 2005. Already people ask me how I got this damn limp. I want you to know I'm not mad. No one knows anything. Not in DC or Phoenix or Tampa or Houston, not in Green River. Not then, not now, not as we ripped Hussein's statue down, not as I stand on a Samarra street corner like some useless traffic cop and stretch my left leg. My mom used to give you shit about butchering English, about saying *preemptive* as if you were some fortune-teller, but she was wrong. I like *preemptive*. Who gives a fuck that we didn't find WMDs? My whole life is preemptive. I didn't wait until cystic fibrosis killed my sister to say *I love you*. I didn't wait until the meth took my father's teeth to say *stop*. I didn't wait until I was goddamn homeless before walking into the recruiter's office. I'm not saying don't do your fucking homework, but come on, you know it doesn't matter why we started the war, no one is clean. You should go out to Rwanda. I hear there are skulls everywhere. You should go out to Utah. Dirt everywhere. You'd like it there. We don't give a fuck about anything but the Weather Channel and Utah winning football games. You come out and I'll show you my old neighborhood and you'll know why Iraq didn't sound so bad. Come out and I'll take you south of town. I know where there's a rope swing out over the Green River. We got to be careful because there's a big fucking rock just below the surface of the water. You can't see it when you're standing on the bank, rope in hand, ready to rock and roll. Come out in August and we'll go watch some stupid fuckers crack their heads open. I'm serious. You'd think that the word would get out, that folks would move the rope or swing out to the right, away from the rock, or at least do as you're taught, to check the depth before you jump, but no one does. Sometimes whole afternoons go by and no one gets hurt, these ignorant fucks just loving the summer life, learning the wrong things, every day, all day, but sometimes a dumbass will launch out just right and take that rock to the body. Come on out and we'll make up some medals for their ambulance rides. Instead of Purple Hearts we'll call them Green Lungs or Orange Kidneys and we'll stick a portrait of Saddam on there and confuse the fuck out of everyone. Or better yet, skip Utah and come on out to Samarra. Come stand with me on the corner. You don't have to do anything different than I do. I'll even dress you up just like me. Come stand with me for a while, for twenty minutes, during rush hour. We'll try to ignore the stares, the Toyotas that stop close, the children's laughter behind us. You'll have to keep those eyes open, George. You blinked once and you got that Iraq pussy, that Samarra pussy, and here I am. I know it doesn't feel good, especially now, but you woke up today and put me on the street corner. Catch a plane and stand with me. I'll wait. Let's make an appointment, and afterwards we'll undress and shower off the sand and sweat and sit down and watch your press conference on TV. We'll see you there on the big screen: nervous as shit, trying to explain that there's such a thing as winning in Iraq. We'll listen for it, but you won't say *preemptive* or *Green River*. That was years ago. We'll see you there and we'll laugh because we know too much now. We'll laugh because there's nothing else to do after you've survived another day in Samarra. There you are, George, in primetime: a red tie, shrugging your shoulders, a Texas smirk, sincere as shit. I believe you. You want me to come home clean.

The Price of Everything

Once, when you were two, your mom and I emptied our savings account to put new carpet down, and the beige Stainmaster still had that new smell that made me think I'd won something. In you came bare-assed and squint-eyed making for the corner of the living room, but no one noticed you right away because Kobe was destroying the SuperSonics on TNT and your mom was off meditating for world peace, so when I heard your grunt I ran to you and I cupped my hands just in time. I carried the warm mess to the toilet and flushed it away and washed my hands, but the shit smell took hours to leave. I soaped up and rinsed five times, but it stuck to my skin. I brought my hands to my face an hour later during another Kobe fadeaway and there it was. That smell: it was love. That shit smell fading from my hands two hours later as I bit into a Taco Bell burrito and knew my life was forever fucked. Love. Hearing your mom bitch me out about the burrito, how the fake meat, fake cheese, fake sour cream would kill me more surely than a return to Afghanistan. Hearing her tell me I should have just let your shit hit the floor on account of the Stainmaster and realizing she was right. Listening to your unrelenting screams over the announcers during Durant's second-half rally and choosing to not load you up and drop you off on a street corner in Sacramento.

All of it—love.

The beige carpet was before the divorce, when your mom still lived with us in Chico. We rented a crappy little two-bedroom apartment three blocks from Bidwell Park that you'll never remember. We had a white Toyota Camry flirting with 150,000 miles and a light green refrigerator and a ceiling fan in the living room that wobbled when we got it going past "low." I had just given up playing basketball in the city rec league—the only time I had for myself—because your mom was headed toward batshit crazy. I'd wake up at night and find her gone, off to the park early in the a.m. to go swimming at One-Mile while the nearby meth heads jacked off on the merry-go-round and monkey bars. At first, I didn't know she was crazy. Back then, in the beginning, her midnight escapes felt eccentric and sexy, and she'd get home in her soaked Chico State hoodie and spout some stupid shit from *The Prophet* or *The Aquarian Conspiracy* and I'd nod along. Almost every time she'd ask me if I wanted to shower with her and I'd say yes and I'd soap her body with a bar of Irish Spring then feel her do the same to me. The first few times she swam at the park I didn't care because I knew she could handle herself, and what's the big deal if she wanted to swim in the dark? Who cares that she wants me to eat better or that she thinks that the fucking Taliban have some not-so-bad qualities? There are worse things.

My biggest fears, then, were that I'd lose my job at Broadway Pawn or that your mom would get pregnant again. I remember the summer being the hottest on record and the sinking feeling I had when the temp broke a hundred and I pulled the ceiling fan cord twice.

You'll hear that your mom and I met through friends in 2002. While that's accurate, it's not the story. I met your mom at a Third Eye Blind concert in San Francisco, high on ecstasy. She wore an Oakland A's T-shirt and had dyed her hair red. Later that night she gave me her number and a handjob a block away from the Fillmore on the tennis courts at Raymond Kimbell Park. The drugs and handjob don't mean we didn't fall in love. Or meet each other's parents. Or make a mistake and move up the coast after my deployment with the National Guard. That doesn't mean that when we found out that your mom was pregnant with you three years later we weren't pissed off, thrilled, and scared. We were.

One day you'll want to know why we divorced. If I have the courage, I'll tell you the final straw was when your mom bit my dick, but I won't. I'll skip that part and my confession that I asked her to bite me during sex, but never below the waist, that every now and then your mom would beg me to call her Madonna. No, I'll tell you about other disagreements, the daytime arguments about me working too much, your mom wanting to live closer to her loser parents in Fresno, her certainty that I killed the wrong people in Afghanistan. That stuff didn't matter, at least not to me. What wasn't forgivable was the day I got a raise at the pawnshop, the evening rain stopping for my walk home, a couple Sierra Nevada IPAs for me and your mom, your mom's mouth around me, my eyes closed, the staggering pain, your mom's bizarre laugh, my fist cracking her temple.

After we both calmed down we agreed not to call the cops. Your mom wrapped ice cubes in a washcloth and pressed it to her face. I dropped four Aleve, cleaned myself up, and slathered some Neosporin on the bite marks. We listened to hear if you were awake, but you didn't make a sound. Your mom went to the park, then came home and called her parents. I could hear only her side of the conversation, her "I'm innocent" voice repeating "Yep, yep, yep." But I knew damn well what your grandfather was saying: *"Darnell was always a loser, even before the war, it isn't your fault, honey, he's just a fuck-up."* Your grandparents always believed everything your mom told them, even the lie that I oversold my headaches to get a Purple Heart. What could I do except hate all of them?

So when it was time to divorce, who got custody of you? The stable father that works his ass off or the freak bitch that thinks a dragon rules the earth? Here's what the judge heard about me: Afghanistan War vet, Zoloft, my fist to your mom's face, one year of ball at Butte Community College, atheist, doesn't read *Goodnight Moon*, an IED outside Kandahar, Purple Heart, Cymbalta, crass motherfucker, likes to be bit during sex, hates vegetables, psycho Sacramento Kings fan, wants the bite as he comes.

Here's what the judge didn't hear: I catch my daughter's shit in my hands and don't raise my voice, I take off your mom's soaked hoodie and towel her down after our shower and call her Madonna, I hold it in when Pierce drops 35 on the Kings, I sell scratched Stratocasters, china sets, and silver handguns so I can walk the aisles of Safeway and throw apples and Doritos in the cart.

I could've had you every other weekend, but why? That's the great big question in life, but there wasn't, and isn't, a why. That's what your mom was searching for in *The Prophet*, but there's no answer as to why I thought "Semi-Charmed Life" was genius, why your mom strolled to Bidwell Park at midnight the first time and decided to take a swim, why she bit down on me, why nine months before you were born I didn't pull out earlier on a beach outside Eureka.

The truth? I didn't want you. Not then. Not when your mom married that asshole from Red Bluff a year after the divorce and your grandparents paid for the fucking lavish wedding. Not when I heard that you were asking for me, wondering if I could come to your tap-dance recital. I was happy, and it wasn't just the little things, it was the second-to-second freedom that convinced me I had my life back. The quiet everywhere, the green Jeep with no room for a car seat, the lavender candles I kept burning, guilt-free rec league on Tuesday and Thursday nights. It was the type of freedom that you never regret: fucking a bar pickup on the living room floor to R. Kelly, the pure joy of Sunday morning boredom before 49ers games, Domino's pizza and a little weed on Monday nights.

I got the call during a Kings game just after Ron Artest tried to pick a fight with the entire Utah Jazz team. I was high and had $200 on the Kings so I let the phone go to voicemail as the crowd applauded Artest's ejection, but when the same number popped up again I answered. A woman's voice told me your mom and the asshole from Red Bluff were dead. They were out on a date-night cruising down Highway 99 when a big rig blew a tire and caught them head-on. The voice on the phone paused, and I don't know why, but I wanted her to keep going with the details. I looked at my arms while she spoke and they seemed massive. The woman kept speaking words but I was looking at the muscles in my arms and listening to the crazy sound of my heartbeat. Then, she said your name, but she didn't say it right. "Manda," she said. "Your daughter." And I pictured you in your mom's house with the baby-sitter. I said, "Amanda, not Manda." I pictured you there, unaware, sleepy, waiting for your mom to return. "Yes," the woman said. "Amanda," and you were mine.

That first night back with me you slept in my bed with your pink and white-checkered blanket because the other bedroom had my weight bench, my old Army shit, and an oversized Pioneer stereo system in it. You fell asleep right away and in the morning I was amazed when you acted as if there wasn't a thing wrong in the whole goddamn universe. You asked for a banana, but all I had was oat-meal, and you ate the whole bowl after I put some honey in it.

Soon, your grandparents wanted to visit, but I told them to fuck off. They threatened to take you away, but what judge would think Fresno was better than Chico? Who would want you running with the Mexicans as California dries up? Who cares if your grandfather is some goddamn dentist fixing the world's cleft palate problems? What does that have to do with anything? They said I had no idea how to raise you, but they were wrong. I bought you clothes and took you out for ice cream and let you pick which cartoons to watch. I went to you during thunder-storms and nightmares. Fuck Fresno.

When I took the nonpaying gig as an assistant coach for the girls basketball team at Pleasant Valley High your grandparents were certain I was screwing all the players, and nothing I said or did changed their minds about me.

Not when we won section championships in 2012 and 2013, or when we sent a girl on a full ride to Cal and another to Santa Clara. Not when the *Enterprise Record* ran a half-page article on my full-court match-up press and my time in Afghanistan. The piece made it sound like I was a goddamn hero for making it out of Kandahar alive then teaching local girls the proper way to trap in the corners. In the photo that ran with the article I'm smiling in my PV polo shirt and holding up my Purple Heart.

It's true that Helena played for me, but I didn't touch her until a year after her graduation even though she kept smiling at me and reminding me she was a year older than the other seniors. She'd leave her hair wet after her locker room shower and walk by me to make damned sure I smelled her cheap perfume, and what did I do? Absolutely nothing. She dropped out of Sacramento State after two semesters because her dad got sick, and soon she was coming into the pawnshop all the time and I'd make her laugh and she'd tell me how she'd never work the almond orchards or rice fields, that she'd start up at Chico State the next year. She always asked about you, and the first time she spent the night she gave you a stuffed giraffe you named "pirate."

On weeknights, you came with me to basketball practices where you dribbled your mini-basketball at the far side of the gym and brought me my dry-erase board when I needed to diagram a play. With each passing season you grew to know the game, and sometimes I forgot that you were just a child when you nodded along to my pregame prep talks. You travelled on the school buses with me to away games and filled the water bottles before tipoff, and on the return drives home you fell asleep on me. I looked out the window at the night and felt your head in my lap. Somehow, I didn't want a different life.

Most days I picked you up from school and you came with me to the pawnshop. You loved that I knew the price of everything. You listened while people broke down and gave me their shit for nothing. You saw me hand some grandma $50 for a string of pearls worth $400. You watched as I rubbed my face before selling a plastic Buddha to some idiot for $100 because I mentioned that Boz Scaggs might have owned it.

When it was slow we played a game where I asked you to pick out your favorite thing in the store and you always surprised me with your choices, like the times you chose a scary Japanese porcelain doll, a bright blue hookah you mistook for a lamp, a busted up drum kit, a pink pellet rifle. Every time you asked me to play the "favorite thing" game you got frustrated because I always pointed above the register to the Montana-Rice-Lott autographed poster celebrating the Niners'89 Super Bowl.

Sometimes Helena came to the store before closing and I locked up and we all walked home together through Bidwell Park. When it was light enough we stopped at One-Mile and you peeled down to your underwear and jumped in at the swimming area. Even at six years old you could swim across at the wide part, no problem. I watched you swim back and forth, watched you lift yourself from the water, watched you and your shitty cannonballs and a dive you called "the twisty bonk." Helena would squeeze my hand or say, "She's swimming better," or tap her foot impatiently. The oaks seemed taller in summer, and although I hated the feeling, nothing I did could fight off the damned memory of your mom.

Your grandparents will tell you that I didn't know how to raise you. You'll hear it over and over. No one will remind you that you asked me to come to your first grade class for "Parent" day, or that I was pissed as hell that all I would get were questions about the war. I was certain everyone had seen the newspaper article on me. You won't remember how you stood in front of your class and introduced me, not as your dad, but as the guy who knew how much everything cost. You didn't even let me give my crappy speech that day. You told your class to pick anything in the world. "Ask him," you said, and when someone shouted "eraser" you looked at me and waited and I said "fifty cents." Someone said, "a jet," and I said "five-hundred million," and that just opened the floodgates, one thing after another: "scooter," "baseball bat," "the moon," "an ice castle," and I answered them all. You stood by me the entire time. No matter what anyone tells you, you were proud.

Make no mistake, you were still a burden, only less often. When a buddy wanted to jet for the coast or a Niners' game on short notice, or when Helena and I wanted to get especially freaky, I had to make sure we had a plan for you, and when I couldn't manage a babysitter or when you wouldn't fall asleep at night, the "I can't" that left my lips killed me each time. And there were many more moments when I wished your mom alive, moments I hoped for that resurrection so you could return to her. When the school said you had lice and I had to drop money on expensive shampoo. Repeated ear infections. You asking about when you could see your fucking grandparents. You refusing to drink milk or sit damn still for more than ten minutes. Your constant begging for dance lessons. A fucking cavity at seven.

But on winter Saturday mornings you had your youth basketball games, and I coached your team and cheered you on as you fucked-up the other seven-year-olds. Best damn thing I've ever seen was you blowing by those helpless shits time and again. The other parents looked at you like some kind of athletic freak, but they didn't know we stayed after the high school practices to shoot hoops and work on your left-hand dribble. They didn't know you watched the Kings games with me and shook your head and yelled at the screen when DeMarcus Cousins melted the fuck down. They had no idea how to love their uncoordinated kids. That's their fault, not ours.

Last spring at your parent-teacher conference your fat-ass second grade teacher asked me if I was concerned you couldn't read like the other kids, and do you know what I said? "No." She wore too much damn perfume and she eyed me like I was some fool. She didn't know that I read encyclopedias as a kid or that the National Guard wasn't my last option. She didn't know that I chose to work in the pawnshop or that it fucking paid better than her job. She asked me if I was providing a "learning environment" for you at home, and I damn near laughed. When our talk was over I looked around the classroom and saw your picture of a two-headed horse and read a sheet of paper where you wrote "bats" after the question "What scares you?" I knew you were fine.

And still, your goddamn grandparents, threatening me, keeping their fucking attorney on my ass. Helena convinced me to let them visit. She was taking a psychology class at Chico State and thought she had mankind's problems solved. "Give them a few hours with her," she said. "They'll see she's fine." Helena had it all figured out. In her dream world your grandparents would come and take you to the park or out to Chipotle, and they'd bring you home and the earth would continue to spin and things would be fine. And maybe, if everything went well, they'd back off.

So they came and got you on a Sunday morning, and your grandmother had the balls to say your mom's name to my face. I never talked shit about them while you were around so you went to them right away. You let them think you wanted them. I hated their smug-ass faces just before they pulled away. I went inside and tried to watch the Broncos destroy the Raiders in the early game. Helena paced the living room till I told her to chill the hell out.

"It's not your problem," I said. "Find something else to solve."

I thought she might cry, but she grabbed her things and left.

After your grandparents dropped you off you came in and stood in the living room and I saw you were wearing new Nike shoes. I asked what you did, but all you said was "talk." When I asked where you went, all you said was "around." When I asked if your grandparents told you to keep everything you did with them a secret you said "no." I let you walk to your room and left you alone. That was love. Not going to you and demanding that you tell me every which way your grandparents fucked you up. Love.

Later that night, you came out of your room and stood naked in front of me. The light of a princess nightlight we kept in the living room was on your feet. "Where's your jammies?" I asked. I was washing brownie crumbs off of our dishes and I worried that you were sleepwalking, but you looked right at me, wide awake. Your arms were at your sides. I thought you would say "Daddy" or "I can't sleep," but you asked, "Did you kill someone?" I let the water run. What was I supposed to say? Was it wrong that I didn't answer? That I lifted you up and took you back to bed?

The answer to your question is "Yes." The truth is I deserved the damn Purple Heart. I had migraines for years after the IED, but they eventually disappeared, so I had to fake one every now and then or no one would believe that they were ever real. The answer is "Yes," I went to war, and I hope I killed more than the two fucks I know of, but most of the time you can't tell. You're firing from behind a wall or a tree and you're just spraying those bullets like crazy. I won't lie and tell you I remember everything about the two I took down. One had a hole in his stomach and was wearing worn-out Reeboks, and one was missing the left side of his head. But here's the important thing. I'm not ashamed of what I've done.

I'm not ashamed that I came home from Afghanistan with a clear conscience. I don't guilt myself when some damn rainy day jacks me up and I pull out the scrapbook and reread my newspaper article or look at pictures of your mom and me. I don't care that that everyone knows Helena played for me. And after I bitched about your mom to Helena, it didn't mess me up when in the middle of sex she said, "Call me her name," and I did.

I don't regret letting you pick your outfits for school or ignoring your grandparents' dickhead lawyer or taking the job at the pawnshop. I knew I couldn't sell other people's shit forever, but for some reason everyone stopped buying guitars and plastic Buddhas all at once even though pawns are supposed to do best in tough times. Even the dumbass college kids stayed away. The owner of Broadway Pawn gave me an extra $20 the day he told me I was done. The next week you came to see me stand behind the counter at the Jack in the Box, and you unloaded your backpack, but the prick manager wouldn't let you hang out. I would've told him to go to hell if I could have afforded to. When I said you had to go home, right then, you didn't move. I had to say, "Don't make me, Amanda," but you wouldn't budge, and I had to grab your arm hard and yank you up. You said, "You're hurting me," but you left me no choice. Can't you understand that? And the next day, when you wanted to wear a sleeveless dress to school so everyone would see the bruise I left on you, what did you want to happen?

You'll never know that most days after work I smelled like shit, grease, and dead cow and I'd walk to Bidwell Park to curse my life. This was no symbolic shit. I wasn't connecting with your mom. I didn't want *The Aquarian Conspiracy* to fall out of the sky or Third Eye Blind to fucking appear mid-chorus. I was angry, but when I looked back on my life and smelled my disgusting skin I couldn't think of a single choice I'd reconsider even though I knew I'd made hundreds of the wrong ones.

By June you were spinning the basketball on your middle finger and kept the ball moving in your hands when we settled down into the evenings after dinner. I joked that the UConn and Tennessee coaches would be calling any minute. You'd hold the basketball on our couch and tell me that you were convinced that you were going to be six foot even though your mom was five-three and I have to stand tall to hit five-ten. When the phone would ring I teased you and said, "It's Geno looking for a six footer." You said you were going to skip college and go straight to the NBA, screw the WNBA, and I thought back to Eureka, to your frantic mom pissing on a third pregnancy test then saying, "Going to be a boy."

You sat next to me on the couch as LeBron James cramped up in Game 1 of the NBA Finals against San Antonio. When LeBron took a guy off the dribble and finished strong, then had to be carried back to the bench, you said, "Dad, he's faking." You wore a blue *Frozen* shirt and were eating an ice cream sandwich, your mouth wide like mine. A commercial came on for the new *Transformers* movie and you took a bite of your ice cream sandwich and stared at me. I nodded and you smiled. I don't know what it was about that smile, but I knew that you were willing to forgive all of my fuck-ups, no matter what happened.

After the game Helena came over. You were sleep. We heard the rain outside, and we locked the bedroom door. We went into the shower together, and I sat down and she stood over me. "You want my piss," she said. Before I spoke the thunder started up. I knew you would be scared, so I said, "Wait a second," and she did. I reached for the Ivory soap as the lighting flashed, and I only got to three before the boom. I listened for your footsteps, your knock, but you didn't come to my door. I thought about going to you, but I stayed there and closed my eyes. I listened until Helena said, "She's okay." I listened a while longer until she said it again, "She's okay," and I believed her.

I knew you would be going to live with your grandparents when I pulled you out of school midday and took you to your mom's grave. I had to take you there before your grandparents got their hands on you. That was love. We drove past the Jack in the Box, past the almond groves out on Midway, and got out of the car. In the south valley we saw the smoke from the burning rice fields. We stood at your mom's grave and you read her name out loud and repeated her middle name, Marilyn. You asked me about her bones, and I lied to you when I said there was a heaven because that is the best lie anyone can give a kid. That's real love. When you get older, if you want to believe your mom is kicking it up in the clouds go for it, but it's not true. If you want to believe your mom died because God took her, you're a fucking idiot. A nail on Highway 99 popped a tire and your mom was flattened. That's the story. But it doesn't matter what you believe, she'll haunt you either way.

You'll never hear how hard I fought to keep you. Your grandparents will tell you I did nothing at all, that I had no representation at the custody hearings, that I wasn't willing to discuss their visitations, that I left them no choice. Believe what you want to. There are no easy answers anywhere. No one's at fault. Years will pass and you won't remember if you chose them or me, or if your opinion mattered at all. I didn't bother asking why the judge decided what he did. You're eight, what are you supposed to know? Who are you supposed to believe?

I'll see you every other weekend, and maybe that's enough. I'll take you to Sacramento Kings games, and we'll eat too much and watch DeMarcus Cousins melt the fuck down. Each time I see you I'll ask if you're growing, and if you top out at five-five I promise I won't say a word.

My fears now are that you will live your life thinking you'll see your mom again, that you'll stop practicing basketball or let someone else take you to games, that one day you'll think I killed the wrong people.

Three days ago, your grandfather picked you up in a Toyota Tundra with running boards. It was hot as hell out, and he had his slacks pulled up to his goddamn neck.

I told him he better not take one step on my front porch. He smiled his perfect teeth at us. You and I stood in the entrance together and you held your basketball. He called out to you. "Manda," he said, and you went to him. You didn't wait or reach for my hand or stop halfway. You didn't look back at me. You acted as if there wasn't a thing wrong in the whole goddamn universe. You hugged him and climbed into his truck.

"Okay," he said, and gave me some bullshit salute.

I opened my mouth, but there was nothing there.

"Yep," he said.

He backed out of the driveway and drove you to Fresno.

I picture you in their ancient living room as they lie to you. I see you wide-eyed on their couch, nodding along. They huddle around you and reach for your hands, and you let them. They tell you that none of this is your fault.

About the Author

JESSE GOOLSBY is the author of the novel *I'd Walk with My Friends If I Could Find Them* (Houghton Mifflin Harcourt), winner of the Florida Book Award for Fiction and listed for the Flaherty-Duncan First Novel Prize. His short fiction and essays have appeared widely, including *Epoch, Narrative Magazine, TriQuarterly, The Literary Review, Pleiades, Salon,* and the Best American series. He is the recipient of the Richard Bausch Short Story Prize, the John Gardner Memorial Award in Fiction, and fellowships from the Hambidge Center for Creative Arts and Sciences and the Sewanee Writers' Conference. He serves as the Acquisition Editor for the literary journal *War, Literature & the Arts.*

A US Air Force officer, Goolsby earned a Bachelor's degree in English from the United States Air Force Academy, a Master's degree in English from the University of Tennessee, and a PhD in English and Creative Writing from Florida State University. He is an Associate Professor of English and Fine Arts at the United States Air Force Academy in Colorado.